Dr N. Dilip Kumar is a socially committed IPS officer who retired as Special Commissioner of Police, Delhi. Apart from contributing to several area of policing, he made a mark for his relentless crusade against corruption. He firmly believes that unless a strong and independent Lokpal and Lokayuktas are instituted, India cannot get rid of the scourge of corruption.

THE NEW AGE OF BAKASUR

N. DILIP KUMAR

SPEAKING TIGER

SPEAKING TIGER BOOKS LLP
125A, Ground Floor, Shahpur Jat, near Asiad Village,
New Delhi 110049

First published by Speaking Tiger Books 2023

ISBN 978-93-5447-395-1
eISBN 978-93-5447-396-8

10 9 8 7 6 5 4 3 2 1

Typeset in Dante MT Std by SÜRYA, New Delhi

Printed at Shree Maitrey Printech Pvt. Ltd., Noida

Contents

Author's Note

For ages, people have been forced to remain the subjects of rulers—kings, dynasties, despots and usurpers. Today, they have the power to be the rulers through democratic means. Yet, unwittingly, they pave the way if not for kings, surely, for usurpers and dynasties, for criminals and cronies, for whom the voters at the bottom of the food chain are non-existent entities. This tragedy is repeated election after election.

One gets a feeling of déjà vu. In the decades after 1947, every regime that came to power in India has been guilty of the same lapses. Abandoning lofty ideals, ethical values and the spirit of sacrifice, the nation has plummeted into a dark age and is suffering—values lost, economic growth hampered, development hindered, the gulf between the rich and the poor ever-widening; and people, deprived and disillusioned, losing faith in the government.

Some resort to radical politics out of despair. There is degeneration and decay, dishonesty and insatiable greed for riches, squabbles for power and colossal corruption all around.

Yet, the masses are confused even when they witness several leaders neck-deep in massive scams—the fodder scam, JMM bribery case, Cash for Questions, Taj Corridor, etc., and several cases of disproportionate assets. Like lambs, they rally behind these corrupt leaders and catapult them to power again and again. It never dawns on them they are declaring these modern-day Bakasurs who strangle the executive, bend the rules and amass huge quantities of illegal wealth to be honourable gentlemen. Blindfolded, the masses do not perceive such greedy men as master criminals. Alas! Instead of saying *sayonara* (goodbye) to their leadership, they simply say, *chalta hai* (it's okay).

Some people have raised their voices and also made quixotic attempts to fight against the odds. But, enfeebled in the course of time, they are ensnared by the bloated monster of corruption. Patriotic songs like '*Dil diya aur dard liya/Aye mere pyare watan*', only serve to break their hearts with deep nostalgia and lyrics like '*Kahan gaye...kahan gaye/Koi lauta de mere beete huye din*' plunge them into nightmarish helplessness.

However, when anti-corruption activist Anna Hazare and public figures like Kiran Bedi and Arvind

Kejriwal and others took the lead a few years ago, many heaved a sigh of relief. With soaring hopes, many joined them and managed to turn the campaign into a massive agitation that awakened the nation with the audacious demand for a strong Lokpal Act that would overthrow the established norms of dishonesty. And, treating this as the second freedom movement, common people began to dream of a nation liberated from the clutches of corruption. It would be the key to real development, they hoped.

One can imagine how anxiously they must have witnessed the drama that ensued. The political class ganged up; made empty gestures of enactment and delayed the process with debates. Session after session of Parliament was adjourned without any good reason, while they pulled the wool over people's eyes with their fake support for the law, and cleverly sowed the seeds of dissent among the leaders of the agitation. The spontaneous agitation was finally tamed, and any tangible action against corruption once again became a distant dream. The voters once again had to face the fact that they had elected leaders, who were elated that they could hoodwink the nation with their devious designs, and who like Nero, arrogantly fiddled while proclaiming, 'We are the Parliament. We are Supreme. The country is totally at our mercy.'

Till India is able to inflict a substantial cost on the Bakasurs, who have a free rein in society (this starts right from the heart of the administration), it is highly unlikely that they would mend their ways. Ultimately, the *laissez faire* of corruption should end. Joseph Pulitzer rightly said, 'There is not a crime, not a dodge, not a trick, not a swindle, not a vice, which does not live by secrecy. Get these things out in the open, describe them, attack them, ridicule them in the press and sooner or later, public opinion will sweep them away.' Society should bounce back again. It should be resilient enough to look for alternatives.

But how? Who will be the redeemers? Clueless, many are searching for the answers, oblivious to a potential alternative available right in their own backyard. We have forgotten the youth, who will soon enter the realm of responsibility, armed with their unadulterated minds. Imbued with values, enlightened about existing reality and the need for change, and with Pulitzer's words as the bottom line of their philosophy, they could certainly be the game-changers we so desperately need.

The purpose of this book is to remind all the honest citizens of India about the role of the youth. Educating young people and inspiring them to take up the cudgels for the future of the country was on my mind when I wrote this book. This is why I have interspersed the story with several real-life examples of dishonest practices, which symptomize the rot everywhere, across cities, small towns and villages in India. They may seem to be depressing. But the intent and endeavour are to use them to exhort the youth to become bold, responsible and value-based drivers of change so that in the course of time, they would guide those who are younger than them, and also confront and correct their elders if they are errant and dishonest. This book is my attempt to convince them that they should mock the corrupt and scoff at those who enjoy illegal wealth like how pigs relish hogging human excreta.

This story of the brothers, Ravi and Pradeep, who come from Bhopal on a holiday to Delhi, and are influenced by the sights they see and the things they hear from their Mamaji, Shekhar, will help, if not all, at least some of the youth, to become agents of change. The hope is that it will also inspire vacillating people to stick to honesty and prick the conscience of some of the corrupt men in our country.

A moot question: why call the corrupt man 'Bakasur'? This book will not only give readers the answer but also persuade them to make sure that 'Bakasur' will become a distinct brand name for the corrupt.

—Dr N. Dilip Kumar

Day One

Suman was on a week's holiday along with her sons at her brother's house in Delhi. After finishing their dinner, they gathered in the sitting room at night. Suman was browsing through some scenes of the *Mahabharat* on LCD. Suddenly, Pradeep told her, 'Ma, this scene is very interesting. Let's watch it.'

Soon, they were all absorbed in the story—a beautiful lac-house was being built by the Kauravas for their cousins, the Pandavas; Vidur, the sane man among them and a well-wisher of the Pandavas, warned them about the evil designs of the Kauravas to set it on fire and secretly helped them to dig a tunnel to escape. This was followed by a scene showing the Pandavas living in the house, each of them taking turns to keep watch in the nights. Then, one night, when it was set on fire, they managed to escape through the tunnel and Bhim carried his mother on his shoulders. The Pandavas reached a village at the end of the tunnel where Vidur was waiting for them with a set of new clothes. They disguised themselves as poor Brahmins so that they could move around incognito from then on. They began to live in the home of a Brahmin, begging for food from the neighbouring houses for sustenance with Bhim getting his share of half of the food since he was always ravenous.

One day, their landlord was downcast and his entire family was crying. When they enquired what was wrong, their landlord told them about Bakasur, the fearsome *rakshas* (demon) who used to prowl around the village and eat people at random. He was so greedy that eating even four or five humans at a time would not satisfy him. Then the villagers had made an arrangement with him. Every day, one member of a family would go to the jungle in a bullock cart taking along with him all the food contributed by the villagers. Bakasur would eat the food, the bullocks as well as the man who brought him the food.

That day, it was the turn of their landlord's family to send a person from the house as food for Bakasur. The Brahmin had to decide whether he would go himself or send his young son to the *rakshas*. The family deliberated about it for long. In the end, the Brahmin offered to go since his young son would be able to look after the family after he was gone.

Hearing about the arrangement with the demon, the Pandavas were aghast. They assured the Brahmin that they would take care of matters. Initially, he was reluctant to accept their offer as he did not want his guests to suffer. But when the Pandavas insisted, he agreed. Bhim was sent to the *rakshas*. While going to the jungle in a bullock cart, Bhim himself ate the entire food given by the villagers. When Bakasur saw that there was no food left in the cart, he was furious. The hungry *rakshas* pounced on Bhim with a vengeance. There was a fierce battle between them. Ultimately, Bakasur was slain and the menace ended.

It was late when Shekhar and his guests finished watching Bakasur's end. They decided to go to bed and to watch the rest of the show the next day.

The train was slated to reach Delhi in an hour. Watching their fellow passengers hurriedly packing their bags, the excitement of the brothers, Ravi and Pradeep, began running high. This was their first visit to the capital. They kept looking through the window at the lights passing by as the train sped ahead. The lights resembled a sea of gold blazing below the dark sky.

In fact, their excitement that began right from the time their trip was confirmed had started bubbling up when they boarded the train at Bhopal. They couldn't stop talking about Delhi—the model mega-city, its malls and historic monuments, all of which they would be visiting. They spoke about their brilliant cousin, Abhi, who was Ravi's age and had just cleared the entrance exam for AIIMS. But most of their conversation was about their Mamaji, Shekhar, who was their hero and icon because of his brave crusade against corruption using innovative sting operations. The media was in awe of Shekhar and covered his crusade in detail.

Hearing the two boys proudly praising their uncle, Suman reminded them, 'How can you forget your Mami, Rekha? She is a lovely person. Unless she and Abhi gave your Mamaji all the support he needed at home, do you think Shekhar would succeed on his own?'

They realized the truth of their mother's words.

Impatiently, they waited to reach their destination, now and then stealing a glance at Suman, who had dozed off on her berth by now.

When the train reached New Delhi railway station, they rushed to the door. The platform was filled with hundreds of people—jostling each other, scurrying up and down to locate their relatives and friends and rushing towards arriving and departing trains. Newspaper vendors, chaiwallahs and sweet-sellers were all shouting at the top of their voices. People were straining their ears to decipher the announcements on the loudspeakers. With their loaded trolleys making clattering sounds, porters cleaved through the crowd shouting, 'Give way, give way'. Everything was noisy and messy.

Peeping out of the coach, they looked for their Mamaji and cousin in the crowd. They spotted Shekhar, who was trying to find a way to reach their compartment. Abhi was a few yards behind, wading through the melee as well.

'Mamaji...Shekhar Mamaji...Abhi...Abhi...' They shouted over the din, waving vigorously at the two.

Shekhar waved at them as he rushed to their door. At the same moment, Abhi too spotted them and excitedly yelled 'hello'. Amidst the coolies scampering around and a sea of passengers, they managed to step out. A coolie with unkempt grey hair wearing a red shirt and sporting a metal license plate tried to whisk them away along with their luggage. Saying no to him and keeping the other coolies at bay, Shekhar and Abhi picked up their luggage.

All of them happily greeted each other as Suman and her sons bent down and touched Shekhar's feet, and Abhi, his aunt's.

'Welcome to Delhi, boys,' Shekhar said, beaming at them.

'Thanks, Mamaji. We are so happy to be here,' they said as their mother fondly looked on.

'Unfortunately, your father had to cancel his tickets because of an urgent official assignment. Otherwise, it would have been great had he also joined us. He's a great entertainer, isn't he? I'll miss him,' Shekhar said.

As the boys nodded, Suman inspected her elder brother closely. 'Your hair's already half-grey,' she grinned.

'What do you expect? I am forty-five. Moreover, there's so much pollution here in the water and in the air,' Shekhar laughed. Brother and sister held hands as they walked on.

Chatting and laughing, the boys followed Shekhar and Suman out of the station. After what seemed like ages, they reached Shekhar's car and stowed away their luggage in the boot. Shekhar sped towards the Ridge area of Civil Lines soon as all of them were seated in the vehicle.

The brothers began their enquiries right away. 'Mamaji, have you caught any big fish these days?' 'Have you caught any gangs taking bribes?' Studious and incisive, Ravi was eighteen and had finished his first year of engineering. One year younger, jovial and bespectacled, Pradeep had finished his twelfth and would also be studying engineering soon.

Abhi chuckled as Suman chided her sons, 'Look, don't distract Mamaji. He is driving. We'll be here for over a week. You'll have time for all your enquiries. Why bother him right now?'

Shekhar assured them, 'I'll tell you many stories. I've plenty of them, trust me!' His wife Rekha had made all the necessary arrangements for the visitors at home. The two boys would share Abhi's large bed and Suman would be sleeping in the guest room. Eager to meet them, Rekha was waiting for the whole party to get home, her pets Bujji, Frooti and Bablu snoozing on the carpet at her feet.

The three pets came rushing to greet them when they walked into the house. Rekha greeted Suman and the boys, while Abhi carried their luggage to the assigned spots in the house. It was a beautiful home filled with carefully curated items bought from artisans who lived in the places where Shekhar had worked. He himself had crafted some of them. Indoor plants also gave the house a warm, homely feel. They flourished thanks to Rekha's green thumb.

Pradeep spotted a framed photograph of his Mamaji in uniform on the wall. 'Mamaji looks very smart in uniform,' he gushed.

The pets followed Pradeep and Ravi everywhere like security guards who were suspicious of their movements.

Abhi did a round of introductions. 'This is Bujji, our golden retriever. She is very well-behaved and warm. The only trouble is that since she is plump, if she lands on your lap, it's very difficult to withstand her affections. Look at our spitz, Frooti. She can sit still like a penguin for hours. Bablu is her cute son from a pom and because of him Bujji gets into all sorts of mischief.'

Abhi shepherded his cousins to their manicured lawn with a prized rose bed at its centre, rows of flowering plants and a fruit-laden jamun tree in a corner.

They went back in at dinner time.

As they were finishing the meal, Shekhar asked, 'Abhi, what have you planned for tomorrow?'

Suman jumped in before Abhi could reply, 'Whatever the programme, first, I'd like to see the sacred Yamuna.'

Abhi nodded. 'Mami, let's drive to the Wazirabad bridge to see your Yamuna *Mata* after breakfast. But before that, let's go for a walk in the morning.'

Suman was happy to agree. And the plan for the next day was finalized.

Day Two

It was almost daybreak. Ravi and Pradeep were jolted awake by a chorus of unfamiliar calls. Abhi, who was already dressed, greeted them with a smile. Seeing their puzzled faces, he explained, 'Oh! These are wake-up calls given by peacocks. It's a privilege reserved for those living in the Ridge area. Otherwise, people in Delhi hear only honking vehicles and the roar of traffic. Come on, get up. Papa is waiting for us.'

They hurriedly got dressed and walked uphill to get to the park. Many cars and two-wheelers were parked outside the gate. Joggers and walkers of all ages had arrived early in the morning to exercise. The four of them walked on, past the people doing yoga in groups. Peacocks were perched on some of the trees. Monkeys keenly watched the people in the park. Monkey families stuck together, picking lice off the bodies of their young. They also saw squirrels chasing each other with their tails up, oblivious of the people nearby.

Shekhar told them how some people collect baby squirrels from their nests even before they open their eyes. Man's cruelty to animals knows no bounds.

Stepping out of the park, they went by the Vidhan Sabha and the civil lines police station before they began their return via Rajpur Road. Here, they spotted a cluster of workers' hutments. There were mounds of garbage on the roadside and they had to cover their noses as they walked past them.

Pradeep shot a riddle at them, 'What has four wheels and flies?'

'Don't ask dumb riddles to Abhi. He is too intelligent. Even I know the answer to this one. A garbage truck,' Shekhar told Pradeep.

They walked on in silence and made a brief stop at the Shiva temple on the way. The priest had lit a stick of camphor and he was ringing a handheld bell as he worshipped the deity. Devotees stood around with folded hands. Watching the worshippers come and go, huge male monkeys stood guard outside the temple gates. With scrawny babies clinging to their stomachs and some riding piggyback, female monkeys flung themselves from one branch to another, clenching bananas in their mouths. The boys watched some monkeys peeling the skin off bananas and eating them. The monkeys stared right back at them.

Pradeep smiled at a monkey and said, 'Hello.'

The monkey bared its teeth in response.

Shekhar asked the boys, 'Should we leave now?'

'One more minute, Mamaji,' said Pradeep who was still engrossed in his conversation with the monkey. His friendliness was going to cost him…

Shekhar started to chat with Ravi and Abhi. When they heard Pradeep shouting, all three of them turned around. They saw a monkey scampering up a tree. Pradeep had been caught unawares. The monkey had jumped on him from behind and before he realized what was going on, his spectacles were gone. The mischievous monkey was now perched atop a branch, fiddling with the spectacles and making faces at Pradeep, who was looking at it helplessly. Quickly, Shekhar reacted. He picked up a banana from a vendor who was parked nearby and lobbed it at the monkey. Rushing to catch the banana, the monkey dropped the spectacles. Pradeep was relieved and he thanked Shekhar profusely for his timely help.

Shekhar said, 'It's fun to watch the monkeys but they are a menace for the entire area, you know. When they invade the housing colonies, they damage plants and flowers indiscriminately. The Municipality workers had an idea and an employee would come here parading a langur seated on his bicycle. But that's not helping anymore. A horde of monkeys attacked the langur one day.'

When they got back home, Rekha was horrified to find layers of soot on their faces. She said, 'Thanks to corruption, Delhi is so polluted.'

Abhi added, 'The air quality is so bad that cancer-causing cadmium and lead have been found in it.'

The boys shook their heads in disbelief and went away to freshen up. They changed their clothes before gathering at the breakfast table.

As he bit into a fluffy idli, Ravi said, 'Mamaji, I really expected that as the capital, Delhi would be a model city. But what I found this morning was appalling. I can't believe it!'

'Like what? Let's talk about it,' said Shekhar.

'The mounds of garbage for example,' Ravi said.

Shekhar said, 'You're right to be surprised. But this is in fact a common sight at several places in the city. And the municipality waits until it piles up, turns into huge mounds and spreads stench and mosquitoes all over.'

'Is there no control over them?' Ravi sounded shocked.

Shekhar looked grim. He said, 'For this, I will have to tell you the story of ghost employees.'

'Ghost employees?'

All eyes were on Shekhar now.

'Well, there was an uproar one day,' Shekhar started. 'The agitated engineers of the municipality gave a notice threatening to stage a *dharna* (sit-in).

Fifteen of their colleagues had been picked up in an early morning swoop by the cops. It had never happened before. A jovial constable tried to cheer up the sulking engineers as he served them breakfast in the lock-up. The shaken Commissioner of the municipality rushed to the Lt Governor with a long face and complained, "Sir, if every engineer is arrested like this, how will I get any work done?"'

'The Lt Governor immediately checked up on the facts. He was informed about the huge fraud in which crores of rupees were being swindled by the engineers and the local politicians in the name of thousands of non-existing employees.'

Ravi asked, 'So blatant? They had no fear of the law?'

Shekhar replied, 'No, they didn't. You can imagine what has happened as a result. The rest of the workers are overburdened. Little wonder that parks are badly maintained and sanitation in the city is only as good as it is in neglected rural areas. You'll be surprised to know how those engineers talk to contractors. They're so clever that they even use coded lingo for collecting bribes. A sting operation caught them in the act.'

'So, what happened to the *dharna*?' Ravi asked.

Shekhar resumed the story. 'Well, with a stern expression, the Lt Governor asked, "Please tell me, Commissioner *Saheb*. Can you ensure honesty on the part of your engineers?" The Municipal Commissioner fumbled for an answer. The Lt Governor gave him a piercing look. "You cannot assure me that you can control corruption in your organization. At the same time, if an officer is trying to clean things up, you are not ready to digest it. Let me be frank, I am happy with what is being done to fight corruption. I do not want to intervene. Better deal with your engineers firmly. If they are not ready to listen to you, go ahead and place them under suspension."

The Commissioner knew it was futile to argue anymore. He mumbled, "Yes, Sir," and left.

That was that. The Commissioner conveyed the decision to the engineers and said his hands were tied. Everyone understood that their *dharna* would cut no ice with the higher-ups and quietly withdrew their agitation. Those in the lock-up stayed there under the watchful gaze of the prison officials.'

Ravi was relieved. 'The LG did the right thing,' he said. 'But Mamaji, it's so sad that after all this came to pass, the garbage still piles up.'

Shekhar replied, 'That's the problem. Only arresting the corrupt is not sufficient. The culprits will not be afraid of anything unless they are punished immediately. Unfortunately, that doesn't happen. They're so accustomed to making money and their complicity is so deep-rooted that they don't wish to find a way out.'

Ravi and Pradeep grew quiet. They were processing what their uncle had just told them.

Rekha turned to Suman, 'You know, at that time, some women's organizations came out in support of the *dharna* of the engineers.'

'Shameless! Perhaps they were instigated by the wives of the men in the lock-up,' Suman ventured a guess.

In a few minutes, they decided to visit the Wazirabad bridge. Suman was the first to rush to the SUV, humming Bhakt Jayadev's *Yamuna teere* (on the banks of the Yamuna) in praise of Lord Krishna.

Abhi smiled at her. 'Mami, you will soon get to see for yourself what your Yamuna *Mata* looks like.'

She cringed as the others got into the vehicle. They drove to the bridge without any more talk of the Yamuna's condition.

The monsoon was yet to reach Delhi. Cribbing about the hot and humid weather, Pradeep squinted at the sun that looked like a blazing white ball embedded in the sky. Ravi glanced at the trees and the greenery as they drove on. When they set foot on the bridge, they saw two blue line buses trying to race past each other. Rekha pulled Suman towards the railing, saying, 'Be careful, they're a real menace here.'

As the bridge vibrated, Shekhar pointed at the water. 'Here comes your sacred Yamuna *Mata*. The poor river is only a ribbon of sludgy and murky water, choked with weeds and offerings of devotees. Look how it is polluted by foul-smelling garbage and effluents from industries and lapping against the shore wearily.'

Suman stared at the river with a dazed look. A heron flew over the water holding a fish in its beak. Shekhar directed their attention to the *dhobi ghat,* the spot by the river bank where washermen wash clothes. Next to it, people were bathing and washing their clothes. Children were scampering around. Pointing at a burning pyre not far from them, Shekhar shared an anecdote:

'Once, an agitated young man came to my officer with a complaint, "Sir, my mother died a couple of days ago and we have cremated her. Yesterday, my brother left for Varanasi to immerse her ashes and I have stayed back to make some arrangements here." The officer listened to him sympathetically.

Tears welling up in his eyes, the young man continued, "When I went to collect her death certificate, the people concerned demanded one thousand rupees. Sir, they only have to take a computer printout and that is so cheap. Though I can afford to pay them, I am deeply hurt. I don't want to give them a penny."'

'What! Even for giving a death certificate, they want a bribe?' exclaimed Suman.

'What do you think? This is a place where nothing gets done without money,' Rekha told her.

Pradeep asked out of the blue, 'Why is there a gate at the cremation grounds? Because people are dying to get in.' He answered his question himself, trying to bring some cheer to the serious faces around him.

Shekhar ignored Pradeep and continued, 'On the face of it, the matter looked small and only two petty officials—one computer operator and his assistant—were involved. Yet, we felt we had to step in and stop what was going on. We set a trap and caught them when they were receiving the bribe. We also ensured that the certificate was issued the same day.'

Ravi was staring at the huge craters in the dug-up sand on the river bank. He asked, 'Mamaji, it looks like people are digging up sand without any checks. Will it not erode the bank and cause floods?'

Shekhar complimented him for his concern. He felt proud of his nephew's powers of observation. 'Certainly, it's a cause of concern,' he said. 'But this is a huge mafia operation. They are active at Bawana and Narela and they have a presence across the country. Though removal of sand without permission is theft, hardly anyone bothers because for every truckload stolen, a special price is paid to the authorities. There have been some agitations but who cares? Even though a sting operation has exposed the sand mafia, nothing much has happened. It stops only for a while and then resumes with more vigour.'

Shekhar explained how the Yamuna gets furious

during the rains. 'It's the poor living on the river bank who suffer while those who swindle her wealth enjoy their spoils. They're very well-connected with politicians, the police and officials of the mining and other government departments.'

Disappointed about the fate of her beloved Yamuna *Mata*, Suman looked crestfallen. 'Let's go home,' she said and started walking towards their car.

Lunch was ready. Still in despair and a bit preoccupied, Suman joined the others at the table. The aroma of the sizzling fish fry Rekha brought in cheered her up.

Shekhar warned her, 'Let me assure you that this fish is certainly not from your Yamuna.'

'How does it matter?' A puzzled Suman asked.

'We should be wary of the fish from the river,' Shekhar said. 'Apart from several pollutants, lindane is found in dangerous levels in the waters of the Yamuna. Lindane is a toxin, a poison that is used in mosquito repellents. Doctors say that it's reaching humans through fish, milk and meat of the cattle and goats that graze on the grass on the river bank.'

'That's scary information, Mamaji,' Ravi's eyes widened. He asked, 'There must be a pollution control authority here? Why doesn't it do something?'

Shekhar said, 'Well, the pollution control authority

is only concerned with filling its pockets with bribes. A good part of the thousands of crores of rupees meant for keeping the Yamuna clean is also swindled. It's a matter of attitude as well. You know, in western countries, polluting rivers and throwing waste in them are considered serious offences. No one is spared there. Here, we say our rivers are sacred goddesses. And yet, we allow them to be polluted and defile them deliberately.'

Suman was heartbroken at the river's plight. Yamuna *Mata* deserved better.

'In spite of all this, your Yamuna *Mata* stays mute,' Shekhar taunted Suman. He added, 'People blindly keep dumping bags of grains and lintels in the river as offerings to the helpless Goddess.' Rekha tried to draw Suman's attention to the big picture. 'Suman, pollution is a very serious problem in Delhi. And so little is being done to address it.'

Shekhar agreed with her. 'Boys, your Mami is right. You have seen the polluted Yamuna with your own eyes. There were many layers of soot on your faces when you came back from a short walk. What more can I say? Delhi is one of the most polluted cities in the world. Fortunately, the courts do intervene now and then. They've helped to introduce CNG vehicles and shunt polluting industries out of the city. But who will treat the people's minds that are afflicted with the toxins of cheating and the lust for wealth? You go to the market. They try to cheat in the name of business. You go to a hospital and you are made to undergo many expensive tests even when you don't need them. Pharmacies sell spurious drugs. This can't be done without the knowledge of the drugs controllers. There is massive corruption in in the municipal Ayurvedic hospitals too. They purchase huge quantities of expensive medicines, which are said to contain gold, for treating critical patients. But these are mostly spurious and have no trace of gold in them.'

'What a capital city!' exclaimed Ravi. Pradeep quietly dug into a plate of jamuns that Rekha passed around. The fruit was fresh from the garden and deliciously marinated in salt and chilli powder. Gobbling up a succulent jamun, he said, 'This is so tasty. And it makes me forget the lousy weather.'

'Don't worry,' Abhi comforted him. 'The monsoon will be here soon.'

That evening, Suman and Rekha went to the Shiva temple. The boys chose to stay at home, playing with the pets who were frolicking on the lawn. Pradeep was amazed at the way they obeyed Abhi's commands as if they shared a language. He asked how the animals had learnt all this.

'Do you know that an average dog is like a two-year child and knows around 165 to 200 words?' Abhi asked. 'Frooti is smarter and may know many more words. Bujji is also very good at it. Bablu, who's still learning, already knows the names of everyone in the house. They've learnt many words on their own; some with small rewards, and a few with gentle punishments.'

Suman and Rekha came home after their temple visit in a while. The two of them were in a jovial mood and having an animated chat. Saying goodbye to them, the boys stepped out for a stroll. On the way, they walked past the rows of temporary sheds which labourers had built on the pavement—held up by bamboo poles, covered with blue plastic sheets on the sides and the top, with forty-watt tungsten bulbs illuminating the inside.

When the boys got home after their walk, Shekhar was drinking his tea. 'How was your day?' he asked.

'Good. We ate some excellent jamuns and played with the pets,' Ravi replied cheerfully. Then, remembering the labourers living in the hutments on the roadside, he mentioned how they had seen the men living there taking a shower under the hoses of the water-tankers.

Looking pensive, Shekhar asked, 'Do you know they take a bath the same way even in winters?'

His nephews were shocked as he went on, 'Yes, they do, since they need to reach their work places early unlike government employees. Using the Delhi smog and traffic snarls as excuses, government employees leisurely reach their offices only after eleven. Then they laze around basking in the sun and drinking tea before settling down to work. Again, after an hour, they rush outdoors to sit in the sun and enjoy a long lunch break. Later, after attending to work for an hour, they hurriedly pack up to leave at 4 p.m., fearing the cold and the smog and the evening traffic jams. This is accepted as a way of life.'

After a pause, he went on to paint a picture of the stark contrast between government employees and labourers. 'A contractor doesn't allow this liberty to his workers. So, they get ready at dawn with the help of their women. Wrapped in shawls, squatting on empty gunny bags, the women make chapattis on make-shift stoves propped up on three stones and fuelled with twigs and sticks collected from the jungle. After a quick breakfast, the men pick up their lunch packs and ride their bicycles to their work sites.'

Rekha added, 'Yet, despite their tough lives, whenever I see them glued to their transistors listening to Hindi songs, I feel that they try to remain content with what they have like the army men posted on the border and the tribes in remote jungles.'

Shekhar was very concerned about the growing inequality in society. 'Look at the wide spectrum—the beggars, the starkest poor, the workers, the middleclass, the rich and the ultra-rich. The gap between the poorest and the ultra-rich in our country—can you imagine it? Some people try to move up the ladder by any means possible. Some government servants accept their position in the social order—high above these workers and far below the rich—as *fait accompli* and take comfort in staying where they are. Others take a shot at becoming ultra-rich by abusing their authority. They are confident that they will get away with it. Even on the rare occasions when the corrupt are caught, there are so few instances of them being punished.'

Shekhar pointed out that the poor remain where they are since all the schemes meant to help them get mired in corruption and frauds. The boys hung on to his every word as he shared some examples.

Shekhar explained, 'We keep hearing about people taking bribes for issuing ration cards and about how low-quality food grains are supplied to people while the good ones are siphoned off to the market. Take the classic example of Arunachal Pradesh. The scheme is meant to provide subsidized grains to people in the remote hills there. Transportation expenses are also borne by the government. In reality, no food grains reach them and the stocks are quietly diverted to the market. At the same time, false claims are made by a coterie of contractors, politicians and officials that grains were transported by trucks from Guwahati to Arunachal and carried by mules and porters to the remote parts.

'The National Rural Employment Guarantee Act is a laudable scheme to provide at least minimum employment guarantee to people. Wherever it is sincerely implemented, people in rural areas get their daily wages for digging wells, clearing paths, maintaining water tanks, etc. But what happens in most places is a different story. People are paid about half of their wages without doing any work while the rest of it is pocketed by those who control the funds. As a result, labourers become complacent. Agriculture suffers a big setback because of this.

'We also keep hearing about children falling sick or even passing away after consuming mid-day meals in some parts of the country. Sometimes, a lizard or a scorpion poisons their meals or some adulterated food items are supplied. Think of the callousness and dishonesty of those in charge!'

In a disgusted tone, he added, 'Such people have no conscience at all. They don't even spare animals.'

'Are you referring to the fodder scam, Mamaji?' Pradeep asked.

Shekhar nodded. 'Can you imagine someone procuring 5 kg fodder for one bird per day? That is the essence of the fodder scam and the scale of embezzlement. People fabricated vast herds of fictitious livestock and procured fodder, medicines and animal husbandry equipment for them. Initially started on a small scale, it grew into a full-fledged mafia operation involving many bureaucrats, elected representatives and business people. Together, they embezzled 950 crores quietly over the years. Although the CBI filed numerous cases, the trials still drag on.'

'There's corruption everywhere, no doubt. But I feel you are scaring the children with all this talk,' Rekha said. She felt sorry for them and hoped they would not turn into cynics after their stay in Delhi.

Ravi assured her, 'Surely not, Mami. It is good to know these facts.'

Shekhar felt that Rekha had a point. He tried to cheer them up, 'Don't be sad. This is simply a fact of life. And you know it has been there since time immemorial.' With a smile, he asked them, 'Have you ever heard of the story of Akbar's corrupt courtier who had gone completely out of control?'

The boys were eager to hear the story.

Shekhar said, 'Fed up with a clever man who was trying to make money by any means, Birbal found him a task that he couldn't possibly profit from,' Shekhar said. 'The courtier was asked to count the waves of the Yamuna every day and send his report to the palace. Of course, in those days it was not polluted.

Cargo and passenger boats were plying comfortably on the river. The man began to perform his duties in earnest while his mind was working over-time on how to make money. And soon enough he found a way. Brandishing the king's order, he stopped the boats from plying, claiming they were preventing him from doing his job and getting an accurate count. No one could question him for that. Slowly, they began to request him for concessions and made lucrative offers in return. He refused to say yes. When they raised their offers, he would agree after a round of bargaining. He was very happy with this state of affairs. This job fetched him much more money than what he had been earning earlier.

'People who commit such malpractices always find a way. In the *Artha Shastra*, Chanakya compared a public servant to a fish in the water and observed: while a fish is in the water one is not sure whether it is drinking or sleeping. So is the public servant.'

There was a smile on Pradeep's face when he heard this. He began to sip the soup Rekha brought in.

But Ravi, who was still brooding over the issue, asked, 'Mamaji, in contrast to the harsh lives of the poor, the rich in Delhi live in the lap of luxury. Abhi says they take their pets to special restaurants. Do they really have so much money?'

Rekha replied, 'Abhi is right. The rich here are so

well-off that they have to constantly find new ways to spend it. I wasn't aware of how they spend a fortune on their pets till an acquaintance of mine invited us to the grand birthday party of their Labrador. Routinely, they take their pets to special pet salons for pedicures, dandruff treatments, etc. Dressing them up in party wear, they hold fancy dress parties where exotic dishes are served. They even get designer clothes for their pets. Only super-expensive tonics will do for their pets, not the ones easily available in the market. We also love animals and we like animal lovers. But the way the rich splurge on their pets and flaunt it is beyond my comprehension.'

Abhi declared like a seasoned philosopher, 'Delhi is a place where the poor live a life of burden and the pets of the rich live a life of luxury.'

Shekhar drank his soup quietly. His tone had a touch of melancholy when he began to talk to them. 'People are so rich that we have heard of a father-in-law presenting a helicopter to his new son-in-law. But the sad part is that their spending spree becomes an infection and ruins many lives. Spending lavishly during weddings has become a status symbol. Even a middle-class man tries to arrange a grand wedding by raising resources through dubious means. He creates a facade of great wealth and goes around boasting about it. The poor man on the street remains a mere onlooker as this brazen display goes on.'

Rekha decided it was time they took a break from the conversation. She said, 'Shekhar, maybe we have given the boys enough to think about. Unless we stop feeding them more stories, they will not be able to digest the special dinner I have made for them.'

Everyone smiled on hearing this. They agreed to talk only about family matters at the dinner table. The meal was delicious. Rekha had outdone herself that day. After they cleared the table, Rekha brought them cubes of ripe bangenappali mangoes from Andhra that were ruling the market at the moment. The season of the famous dasheris was still a few days away.

Later, while they were drinking coffee on the lawn, Ravi goaded Shekhar into telling them another real-life story from his vast repertoire. This one revolved around the greed for illegal wealth.

Shekhar chose to talk about Megha Rani, an influential Commissioner of Income Tax. Her husband was a senior engineer. Financially, they were in a very good position thanks to their double income. Their only son was doing his final year of engineering. But, instead of being satisfied with what she had, the greedy official would demand bribes to settle tax violation cases.

Finally, a case was registered against her. Searches carried out at their residence led to a bank locker, which in turn led to the discovery of some undisclosed properties. One such property was a palatial bungalow which had been constructed in a posh colony. The guard at that place pleaded ignorance when he was asked about the keys of the house. Megha Rani and her husband outrightly disowned the property. Their neighbours, however, secretly confirmed that it did belong to the family.

When she was arrested, she feigned sickness and was rushed to the government hospital since she had fainted. Perhaps she never expected that the doctor there would admit her in the general ward. Unfortunately for her, that did come to pass. Imagine how shocked she must have been! Having been used to living a life of luxury she could never have pictured herself inside a government hospital.

Meanwhile, the lock of the bungalow was broken open. It was empty. There was a room in there that was securely locked as if it needed extra protection. That lock too was broken. Inside the room, the investigating team found two large suitcases with numbered locks. Megha Rani's husband and son pleaded ignorance. When the boy was pressurized and officials threatened to ruin his future career if he did not reveal the truth, he broke down and spelt out the code. When the suitcases were opened, wads of currency notes were found in them. To the utter astonishment of everyone present, the amount turned out to be a full one crore rupees.

Rekha chuckled and added, 'The next day, Megha

Rani sent a message to the investigating officer requesting him to get her shifted to the police lock-up. One day in the government hospital ward was more than enough for her. It felt far worse than any police lock-up.'

Suman and the boys started laughing.

Shekhar added, 'The team readily obliged her, exulting that their trick had worked really well.'

'Mamaji, it's hard to believe that such a senior officer would become so greedy,' Pradeep said.

'That is the tragedy,' Shekhar said. 'In fact, it is the most serious problem plaguing us. If well-paid, well-off senior officers are dishonest, how on earth will the subordinates be honest? The source of corruption originates at the top. Presume for a moment that the Commissioner of Police posts a Station House Officer (SHO) only on a premium. Then what do you expect from the SHO and his men? They'll squeeze the public, won't they?'

Shekhar told them about instances of the police harassing people who were embroiled in dowry cases. He had heard of many senior cops who were neck-deep in corruption and bribery. 'Yet, many of their subordinates remain honest only because of their inherent sincerity. Constables or clerks, hats off to such people! We should be proud of them. They deserve our respect.'

Since it was getting late, he said, 'I think we've had enough for today. Let's call it a day?'

'Mamaji, why do people lust after wealth so much? What will they do with all that money? A person's needs are limited. Are they sick or crazy to be so greedy for money?' Pradeep suddenly sounded dead serious.

Shekhar appreciated his nephew's insight. 'Pradeep, your thinking is absolutely right. Initially, there may be some genuine need and then it becomes a habit. Later, it turns into greed. In course of time, it afflicts a person like a sickness. He goes on changing the benchmark every time he acquires something—one car, more cars; one bungalow, more bungalows; one crore, hundreds, thousands of crores. It's nothing but a pathological condition. It deprives people of sense.'

He added, 'Rightly, it is said that there are only three ways in which wealth can be disposed of—*danam*, *bhogam*, and *nasham*. *Danam* or donating is the best way. *Bhogam* is consumption. How much can one consume? The rest of it will be destroyed through strife and litigation, or will be frittered away on destructive vices. Those who inherit such wealth also become lazy and useless and destroy themselves; *nasham* is inevitable. Such people have zero self-awareness till it happens though.'

Ravi asked, 'Mamaji, their greed for wealth is endless?'

'They are like Bakasur whom you saw in the *Mahabharat* yesterday. Like him, they have a voracious appetite,' Shekhar said. 'These are the modern-day Bakasurs with side-kicks milling around them and god-men blessing them. Corrupt cops bend the rules for them. They tilt the scales of justice in their favour in order to gobble up piles of currency notes. Gandhi must be turning in his grave!'

The boys thought that this was an apt comparison. The modern-day Bakasurs were indeed a grave danger to the country.

Shekhar added, 'Every story in our mythology speaks about the fight between good and evil. They were put together by wise men with a social conscience. Making a selection of all the good traits found in people, they created a few characters who embodied these. Adding a few extravagant flourishes, they attributed godliness to these characters. They also created evil characters and called them *rakshasas* and showed them in all their ugliness—wild hair, horns and brute physical strength. *Rakshasas* were said to eat human flesh and also prey on animals. Please understand; there were no real *rakshasas*. Such depictions were only embodiments of the evil tainting society. Mythological stories give people plenty of role models to worship and emulate like Rama, Krishna, Arjuna and Bhishma. There are characters to loathe too. Bakasur in the *Mahabharat* is one such loathsome *rakshas*.'

'Mamaji, you are right,' Ravi said. 'Henceforth, we will also call every corrupt man Bakasur.'

Suman agreed with them. 'Shekhar, I don't think there can be a better comparison,' she said. 'It should become a brand name for all corrupt men. I'll go back to Bhopal and share this with my neighbours there. I'm sure they'll all agree. Only the men who actually happen to be Bakasurs and their wives will object to it.'

Pradeep asked in all innocence, 'The comparison with Bakasur is very apt as far as their appetite is concerned. But why treat them as *rakshasas* when these men are just corrupt?'

Shekhar clarified. 'First, tell me who a criminal is,' he said. 'A person who commits crimes like theft, robbery, cheating, murder, right? So, what should we call a man who commits serious crimes like those listed under the Prevention of Corruption Act and forgery, cheating, fraud, criminal misappropriation, money laundering, criminal breach of trust, conspiracy, extortion and perjury? What should we call him when he breaks the laws which regulate income tax, import/export and stamp duty? Isn't he a jumbo criminal? Since he commits crimes against society, he's anti-social. Since he commits crimes against the nation, he's anti-national. To phrase it in police lingo, he should be termed a history-sheeter. And speaking in terms of mythology, he is a *rakshas*.'

Everyone nodded. Shekhar was right of course.

Shekhar was livid. 'What's so respectable about

these selfish men who are in positions of power? People gather to hear them giving speeches and sermons on values. If they smile at someone, that person feels special. If they pretend to care about anyone's welfare, people elevate them to the status of saints. Is it just because they have power? Don't you think people are desecrating their lives by shaking hands with such *rakshasas*? When a starving man steals money or food, he is arrested and locked up. A poor man who is forced to become a thief because he is in dire need is punished for his crimes. On the other hand, your "merely" corrupt man has everything—a job, a salary, basic amenities and above all, a sense of security. Yet, he swindles the public, steals their money and takes bribes, presuming it to be his prerogative.'

Rekha joined in. 'A man who had no riches before he entered government service or politics becomes a feudal lord in no time. Nothing but greed drives him and makes him commit grave crimes.'

Suman told her sons, 'Your Mamaji has rightly said that such people are real *rakshasas*. They are the greediest Bakasurs of our time.'

The boys had never thought along these lines but Shekhar had opened their eyes to the truth. 'Bakasur' was indeed the correct name for the corrupt men who gobbled up what was not theirs to demand or covet.

Pradeep, always eager to bring a smile to the

faces around him, shared these words of wisdom with them, 'Some people bring happiness wherever they go. But these corrupt people bring happiness whenever they go. So, they should go...'

Ravi agreed wholeheartedly. He immediately began to make mental notes about friends and relatives who deserved the name 'Bakasur'.

Day Three

That evening, as the sun was setting on the horizon, the boys were engrossed in eating leechis, sinking their teeth into the sweet white flesh after peeling off the prickly skin. Shekhar came in and greeted them. He had gone for a walk, which was a part of his regular daily routine.

When Shekhar settled down on the couch, Ravi said, 'Mamaji, this noon we happened to meet a florist who was all praise for you. He said he is grateful to you for helping him when he was in dire need. He thinks that you strike terror in the hearts of the corrupt. The man is full of admiration for you.'

Rekha guessed the man's name at once. 'Oh! That has to be Tanvir. I remember him.'

'Yes, Ma,' Abhi confirmed.

'Tanvir,' Shekhar said with a smile. 'He's a brave and resourceful soul. Poor man, he was harassed by several people from different departments when he

started a small eatery along with his flower shop at Connaught Place. It was a case of serial harassment and a traumatic experience for Tanvir.'

Pradeep prodded him to tell them the whole story. How had Tanvir survived his ordeal? What part did Shekhar play in rescuing Tanvir from the Bakasurs who stalked him?

When Tanvir started his eatery, he was not given a license in spite of his numerous visits to the work places of the officers concerned. He had done the necessary paperwork but that did not make any difference to the crooked officers.

Shekhar reminisced, 'One day, he came to me with a complaint. Prakash, a powerful inspector (enforcement) in the municipality, was troubling Tanvir constantly. On the one hand, he was not clearing Tanvir's license to run the eatery, and on the other hand, he was insisting that Tanvir should pay him three thousand rupees every month to run it without a license. Tanvir couldn't afford to pay that much.'

Shekhar had immediately sensed that there was more to the story. He told Pradeep to speak frankly. How many officers were demanding monthly bribes from him? It couldn't be just Prakash. Tanvir shared a long list of corrupt officers to whom he was handing over ninety percent of his earnings in the form of bribes. It was destroying him financially and he felt frustrated and totally helpless.

Shekhar went on to give Tanvir certain instructions which were to be strictly followed. A sting was carried out thanks to Tanvir's cooperation. He did a wonderful job of recording his conversations with the crooked officers over a period of time.

The main culprit was Prakash of course. But first, Tanvir recorded his conversation with another Inspector, who was caught on tape saying, 'Do Prakash's work first.' When Tanvir said that he had made the payment on the tenth, the Inspector said that the payment was meant for the previous month. Tanvir would have to make another payment for the current month within a day. He then cautioned Tanvir that in case of any mistake, one message from Prakash was enough to destroy him. No one would be able to help him. Therefore, 'Do his work first,' the Inspector insisted.

Another recording Tanvir managed to procure was with Inspector Prakash. He said, 'For this month, make the payment on Monday. I will let you know through whom to make the payment in future.'

Yet another recorded conversation was with a constable and his colleague who told Tanvir, 'Pay us first, then the SHO, afterwards the Division Officer, and then the head constable. A shop can be run only this way.'

And in another sting operation, the Assistant Labour Commissioner was caught refusing a bribe of

Rs 500, saying, 'Who wants this measly amount? Even a *chaprasi* (peon) would not take it. Keep it with you.'

Recordings went on—with police officials and officials of the departments of labour, health, sanitation, water supply, enforcement of NDMC, etc., who were all caught either demanding or accepting their monthly *haftas* (protection money). They threatened to harass those who failed to make such payments by confiscating their goods and releasing them later at a higher premium. This was a regular ploy of theirs.

Impatiently, Pradeep asked, 'What action was taken finally?'

Sekhar replied, 'Since very clear evidence was available, seventeen officials were arrested on the same day. The media covered the arrests in such detail that it rattled the NDMC administration. The public was watching it all on TV.' Laughing, he added, 'The NDMC Chief rushed to his political bosses for protection. But there was little they could do since the evidence was irrefutable.'

That morning, the cries of peacocks had woken up Pradeep. He sat up in bed, glancing at Abhi and Ravi who were lost in sleep. 'Hello, friends,' he wished the pets when they came into the room, wagging their tails. Bujji licked Abhi's hand and placed her heavy paw on his shoulder. Abhi woke up.

Pradeep proposed, 'Abhi, why don't we take them for a walk?'

'Let's get ready then,' Abhi said, springing up from bed.

After Abhi and Ravi got dressed, they set out for a walk.

Pradeep asked, 'Abhi, how do you manage these pets during the severe Delhi winters?'

'That's no problem at all. In winters, they are extremely happy. They race each other to the room heaters and snuggle up in their quilts at night. Early in the morning, they allow us to dress them in colourful woollen jackets. And when we go for walks, they proudly show them off to the other dogs we run into on the way.'

His cousins burst into laughter.

Abhi grew serious, 'Winters are fine. But it's a hell of a job to take care of them when people burst crackers especially for Diwali. They're terrified and they hide under our beds. Sometimes we have to use earplugs to calm them down.'

Pradeep felt sorry for the pets. There were such carefree, friendly creatures. Why were people so callous towards them?

After their walk, they headed home and had breakfast. The walk had done them good in spite of the polluted air. At around 11 a.m., they stepped out of the house. The SUV was waiting to ferry them across town.

Abhi told the driver, 'Kashmiri Gate, Darya Ganj, India Gate, INA market, Karol Bagh and back home. That's our plan for the day.'

As they got close to ITO, they saw that the road was crammed with hundreds of vehicles. There was bumper-to-bumper traffic. In Bhopal, they had never seen such a rush. Watching the traffic cops, who were inhaling the polluted air and sweating it out in the blazing sun while trying to control the traffic, Ravi said, 'It's a hard life for them, isn't it?'

'It's a thankless job. One small mistake on their part and people pounce on them,' Abhi said.

'While these people are slogging away in the heat, there are policemen out there who are coolly extorting money from innocent people.' Ravi remembered the dowry case their Mamaji had told them about the previous night.

A woman complained to the anti-dowry cell that her in-laws and her husband had been harassing her for dowry. Her in-laws, who were very poor, were summoned to the police station by an officer. At the station, the officer, and his associates—a head constable and a female constable—tried to explain to them how serious the matter was and how they would have to spend years in jail.

The old man said, 'Sir, we are very poor people. And the complaint is false. Unfortunately, our daughter-in-law had an affair with another man and when we objected to it, she cooked up this false complaint.' The officer shut him up and sternly informed him that there was no other option than to file a case and arrest them all. The female constable and the head constable tried to act as if they were the family's well-wishers and persuaded them not to confront the officer. They advised them to give him whatever he wanted if they expected any relief. With some more intimidation and persuasion, the family ultimately agreed to pay twenty thousand rupees. It was settled that no case would be registered.

But soon, they found out that they had been booked. The shocked family confronted the officer. Shamelessly, he changed his stance. Acting as if he was furious, and with a wicked smile on his face, he told them that unless a few more thousands were shelled out, they would make the case even stronger and haul up the minor children in the family.

Aghast, they filed a complaint, and were advised to follow a plan.

Secretly, they made video/audio recordings of the officer and his associates and gathered evidence— about the demand and the promises they had made earlier, and the amount given as bribe and the shares pocketed by each. They also managed to record a conversation about the new demand and the threat to implicate their minor children. Evidence that the police officers were aware of the extra-marital affair of the daughter-in-law as well as her role in framing a false case was also collected.

Plans were then made to trap the officer and his associates while they were accepting the bribe for the second time. They were caught red-handed and booked for corruption and extortion.

~

The car inched ahead and the boys were caught in another traffic snarl soon. Here too, the hapless traffic police were struggling to clear the road. Finding Ravi cribbing and Abhi helplessly staring at the traffic jam, Pradeep tried to lighten their mood with a joke:

He said, 'A patrolling police van noticed a car swerving all over the road. The head constable switched on his siren and pulled the driver over. "You need to take a breath analyzer test," said the cop. "I can't. I have very bad asthma and I may have an attack." "Okay, then take a blood test." "Can't do that either," the man responded. "I am a hemophiliac and if a wound is opened, I could bleed to death." "Ok. I will take your urine sample then." "Sorry, Sir, I also have diabetes and that could push my sugar level really down." "Oh! At least walk in a straight line." "Can't do that either." "Why not?" demanded the exasperated cop. "Well, because that stupid line won't stop moving." The angry cop yelled, "I have stopped the line from moving. Now, you walk." "I can't do it, Sir." "Why?" "Since I'm drunk," the man finally said.'

All of them burst out laughing. Mercifully, the traffic snarl eased up then.

On the way, they had to stop at more than one spot since construction work was going on. The work on the Delhi Metro as well as flyovers created huge jams. Drivers hurled abuses at each other. Everyone honked and there was complete chaos.

At a junction, their driver pointed out the vendors who were hawking coconut pieces to passersby. Some of these were offerings made to the dead at Nigambodh ghat and other cremation grounds in the city, and were collected by the vendors at throwaway prices.

They also came across young boys selling pirated copies of books and magazines, and plastic toys. At a traffic light, they saw clean-shaven eunuchs in female attire—colourful saris and churidars, lipstick and items of cheap jewellery. Their gestures were markedly effeminate.

'Look at them,' Ravi said. 'They are outcasts and society shuns them. They are not considered employable and so they have to resort to begging or live off sex. I feel sorry for them. Society has no right to deny them their humanity. Where are the safeguards of their dignity and their right to work?'

'Survival is a daily battle for these people. Will things ever change for them?' Abhi asked Ravi.

They also ran into beggars on the way—some of them were physically challenged and were living on the streets. An old man in rags, who was coughing badly, limped up to them and begged for money to buy a meal. They saw small children with smaller children tied to their backs and women carrying wailing infants begging for alms. At a crossing, they saw a leper seated on a hand-operated cart. He crisscrossed the gaps between vehicles and asked passersby for money. A careless driver could knock him down any minute.

Pradeep asked Abhi why the government of the capital was not bothered about the poor and the destitute.

Abhi joked, 'They are too busy trying to showcase our achievements to foreigner visitors.' Then he grew serious. 'You must have heard how many officers of the department of social welfare were arrested by the anti-corruption unit. The officers of the department, who are supposed to take care of the destitute and the homeless by providing them food, shelter and clothes were in cahoots with a contractor. Literally, every official procedure required for making purchases was managed by the contractor himself and not the officers. Prices were hiked, low-quality items were supplied or not supplied at all. The fraud went on for several years and the officers amassed many assets.

When the racket was busted, I remember how every one of them tried to hide their faces from the news cameras and reporters.'

Even when the traffic lights turned green, their car could not speed up. Many drivers treated traffic laws and the very concept of safe driving with contempt as if none of it applied to them. Pedestrians raced across the road, signalling at vehicles to slow down and let them pass as if they were traffic policemen. Shocked, Ravi asked Abhi whether Delhi was a modern city or a rustic place. Abhi said he really did not know the answer.

They had another hurdle to cross on the way as well. The expected arrival of a VVIP held traffic to ransom. The road was blocked off and everybody was asked to wait till the VVIP and his convoy drove past. People muttered under their breath. The clock ticked but there was no sign of the VVIP. An ambulance was also in line, unable to rush the patient to the nearest hospital.

Pointing at the ambulance, Abhi said, 'Once I saw a patient being brought dead to AIIMS. The ambulance carrying him was stranded and the man had died on the way. Later, when it was reported in the news, the VVIP responsible for the delay expressed deep regret. But the same thing keeps happening again and again. Regret is just an empty word when you continue to behave in an irresponsible manner.'

His cousins agreed with him. Things were never going to change if this VVIP culture flourished. Why were special privileges accorded to a few at the cost of the common man?

After a long wait, the VVIP and his entourage drove past with the deafening sound of sirens filling the air. Their car picked up speed and drove on for a while but construction sites kept popping up with annoying regularity on the way. Flyovers were being built and roads dug up.

'They cause so much inconvenience to people because construction is being done in such a haphazard manner,' Abhi said. 'Flyovers may ease the flow of traffic in the future. But who knows, by that time, the number of vehicles may multiply. Planning is critical here but that is the one thing that is lacking.'

Another massive traffic jam forced their driver to stop the car. They got out of the vehicle and saw a grim sight. A blue line bus had mowed down a man while recklessly overtaking another bus. The body was mangled and blood was splattered all around him on the road. His face a mess. Some people were standing around cursing the authorities. Everyone at the scene was waiting for the cops to arrive and drive the victim to the hospital. The man's chances of survival seemed slim.

The three of them walked back to their car in shocked silence. Abhi said, 'Damn these blue line buses! They are a curse! Media reports accuse policemen, politicians and transport officials who own many of these unsafe buses and manage to get fitness certificates even without getting their fitness tested.'

'How do they do that?' asked Pradeep.

'A sting operation exposed the licensing fraud of the transport department,' Abhi explained. 'When the sting racked up the evidence, the media reported the facts and shared all the details with the public. Getting your driving license delivered at your doorstep is very easy. Get hold of the touts of the transport officials, pay them their commission. That's all it takes. News channels showed how touts were seen collecting money and papers from the applicants; how driving school instructors were acting as the middlemen between the applicants and the touts; and how the touts in turn would contact the officials who were conducting the driving tests and share money with them. Video clippings also showed how only farcical tests were being conducted. With the driving school instructor sitting by his side, one man moved the vehicle hardly a few feet. Most applicants couldn't even hold the steering wheel properly. People were terrified when they came to know that so many unfit drivers were out there, about to cause serious accidents. The biggest danger was the fact that fitness certificates for vehicles were being issued without conducting any tests. The public was grateful to the anti-corruption officers who busted the racket as well as to the media who covered it.'

Their car circled past Karol Bagh and Ravi asked Abhi, 'Why don't we stop here for a while and go shopping? We could pick up some interesting stuff for ourselves and for the whole family.'

'Shopping here, at this time?' Abhi sounded shocked. 'That's a terrible idea. The driver will have to search for hours to find a place to park the car. If you're so keen to shop, we'll come again, but only by the Metro. That'll save us the hassle of hunting for a parking space, which is a really impossible task.'

Pradeep and Ravi were happy to take Abhi's advice. He knew the city best and they did not want to waste time looking for a parking space in crowded Karol Bagh. They decided to head back home and have a late lunch. Enough driving around for the day!

Shekhar was keen to hear about their day. Which spots in the city had they visited? Had they enjoyed the drive?

'The drive was interesting, Mamaji,' Pradeep said. 'Ravi told us about the licensing fraud on the way. What a scam!'

Shekhar remembered all the details of the sting operation that had shone the spotlight on the racket.

The licensing fraud would have put even more lives at risk had the operation not happened. Shekhar recounted, 'The constable on duty spoke about his conversation with the then SHO who had posted him on the Transport beat. He said, "I told the SHO that I had paid him lakhs of rupees. Suspecting that I had not paid him correctly, he asked for details. I explained that I had paid him Rs 40,000 for nineteen months and that came up to about eight lakh rupees in all." The conversations of some of the touts who were active then were also recorded. They were taped pleading with the leader of the touts, "We have learnt that your Motor Vehicle Inspector takes only Rs 200 per case from some other touts whereas you are charging Rs 500 from us." The leader replied that he himself was paying Rs 500 per case since the Inspector would not discriminate between people when he collected bribes. Since the MLO refused to reduce the amount, the Inspector also could not do so. It was the MLO who bagged the lion's share.'

The scale of the operation was massive. The sums of money that changed hands, mindboggling.

'Mamaji, we also saw a lot of beggars on the way,' Pradeep said. 'Many of them were handicapped people.'

Rekha asked, 'Did you also see children who perform acrobatics at the traffic lights to earn a living? They are risking their lives by doing acrobatics on busy city streets.'

'I was told that children are kidnapped and amputated by racketeers and then forced to beg. Is it true, Shekhar?' Suman asked.

'Unfortunately, yes. There are organized rackets which are actively involved in creating beggars,' Shekhar confirmed.

Pradeep said, 'These vulnerable people are under attack from all sides. Abhi told us how the department of social welfare officials collude with contractors. What a shame that in spite of the arrest of many culprits, the poor have no one to turn to.'

'Sometimes, the police round up beggars and lodge them in the beggar homes run by the department of social welfare,' Shekhar said. 'But they are back on the streets soon enough. Nothing shocking—just corruption as usual! The people who run the homes let off the beggars and falsify their attendance in the official register. The beggars in turn share a portion of their earnings when they come back to the homes at the end of the day. Like Akbar's corrupt courtier, people find ingenious ways of making money wherever they are.' Pradeep, Ravi and Abhi burst into uncomfortable laughter. Shekhar added, 'Unfortunately, the officials of the department of social department enjoy the patronage of the higher-ups and politicians. It was a huge challenge for us to prosecute the contractor and the corrupt officers after they were caught.'

'It seems that touting is a flourishing business in Delhi,' Ravi said.

Shekhar agreed with him. 'Touts galore. They make all the decisions in several government departments. They take a call on who should benefit from government schemes—healthcare, education, housing and other welfare schemes which are meant for the poor. They can brand a rich man of their choice as "poor", and let him milk these cash-rich schemes. These crooked touts can also deny a dirt-poor man the benefits of government dole if he does not pay them a fee.'

Pradeep wondered aloud, 'Are they officers who are meant to serve the people? Or common crooks and extortionists?'

'Well, there are good people in every system,' Shekhar assured him. 'And then there are the Bakasurs who extort money even in petty matters like what happened once in a slum.'

'Which incident are you referring to?' Ravi asked.

Shekhar shared the details with them. 'Ashok who worked as a casual driver lived with his family in one of the numerous slums in Delhi. One day, he was pruning an overgrown tree that was threatening to cause damage to his roof. The beat policemen pounced on the poor man out of the blue.

Tapping his *lathi* (stick), the policeman barked, "Eh! You are cutting down a tree. Have you taken permission from the forest department for this?"

Puzzled, Ashok replied, "No, Sir. I have not

taken permission from anyone. I am only pruning the branches to protect my roof. I didn't know that I needed permission to do this."

The policeman said, "Even so you are committing a crime. We'll have to book you for this offence."

Ashok pleaded, "Sir, how does pruning amount to cutting down the tree? In fact, you can see that the branches are damaging my hut and this is the only option I have."

The policeman was furious. His face turned fiery red and he retorted, "Are you trying to teach us the law? Come with me to the police station. You'll understand what we can do."

Petrified, Ashok spoke to his relative, Surender. He came rushing to the scene to help the hapless Ashok.

Surender also tried to reason with the policeman. But he was adamant and rudely brushed aside his pleas. He bluntly put forward his demand, "If you do not want any police action to be taken, you have to pay us ten thousand rupees."

They were taken aback. Then, realizing the futility of pleading, worldly-wise Surender requested a day's time to make the necessary arrangements.

Ashok and Surender went ahead and filed a complaint against the police and were given instructions about handling a hidden camera which would record their conversations with the police.

They were also given guidelines about how they should conduct the conversations so that proper evidence could be collected.

A group of policemen came to meet Ashok and Surender at a spot they had agreed on. While Ashok treated them to tea and samosas, Surender struck up a friendly conversation.

He requested the head constable, "Sir, we think that ten thousand is too much for such a petty matter. Please try and reduce it."

The head constable exclaimed, "What's ten thousand! Pay up or he will go to jail. We are being considerate because he is poor. Do you know that we are paid thirty thousand rupees usually for such cases?"

With folded hands, Surender pleaded again, "Sir, my relative is very poor and just a casual driver. He doesn't have a steady income. Please make it five thousand."

Ashok, who was standing next to his cousin, joined in. "Please, have mercy, Sir," he begged.

The constable replied, "Look, do you think that the entire amount is meant only for us? Let me tell you how it works—our share is only five thousand. The rest is due to be given to the SHO. Therefore, we cannot reduce it. Trust us. We're being frank with you here."

Pretending that he had given up hope, Surender

conceded, "Ok, Sir, your five thousand will be arranged. As for the SHO, I will speak to him and try to convince him about the amount."

Assured of their cut, the policemen tried to sound generous, "You may try. We wish you luck."

Later, Surender spoke to the SHO on the telephone and recorded their conversation as well.

He introduced himself to the SHO and said, "Sir, do you remember me? My brother was assaulted a month ago and despite the fact that the medical report indicated a grievous injury, no case has been registered by the police so far. Sir, I've already met you a number of times regarding that matter."

The SHO answered after a pause, "Yes, I remember. Let me see what I can do."

Surender continued, "Sir, while your policemen are still hesitating to take action in such a serious matter, your beat staff is too eager to register an offence in this trivial matter. The issue is all about pruning the branches of a tree. In fact, these branches are damaging my relative's hut and he has no choice but to do this. What happens to justice here, Sir?"

"It is an offence, you know," the SHO insisted.

Surender put on a submissive act. "Sir, I don't want to dispute what you are saying. But now, the problem is that they're demanding ten thousand rupees for not registering the case. They say that out of this, five thousand is for you. When I pleaded with them that

I'd talk to you as far as your share is concerned, they were happy to let me try."

The SHO coolly said, "Let me see what I can do."

The next day, when the policemen came to collect the promised amount from Ashok, they were caught red-handed. The SHO had done nothing to stop them. Had he been honest, he would have taken stern action against them. He looked the other way when his men were indulging in illegal activities. Hence, the SHO too was booked for conniving with the greedy policemen.'

Abhi said, 'Papa, I always worry about how when one man commits malpractices, he also protects all those involved in the murky business. It is like the work of an organized gang.'

'You're right, Abhi', Shekhar replied. 'They're birds of the same tainted feather. These Bakasurs literally prowl around in gangs sometimes.'

He shared an example with them. 'Once there was a simple dispute between two neighbours about sharing a common wall. They approached the civil court to settle the matter. While sending legal notices to them for their court appearance, the court also sent a notice to the concerned department for filing an affidavit. They only had to confirm the facts based on their records. That was all. But, the *kanungo* (village officer) of that area sent word to the defendant that he would be visiting him. The man sensed the officer's intentions and rushed to us for advice. We shared a specific plan with him and he made arrangements for making video and audio recordings when the corrupt *kanungo* would come visiting.

'The houseowner was taken aback when the *kanungo* arrived with a gang who claimed they were also *kanungos* from other areas. A group of greedy officials had gathered at the man's house! This was a great opportunity to expose their practices. Each *kanungo* made fictitious arguments to extract money from the man. When he hesitated, they bulldozed him into believing that they would send a favourable report to the court, provided their *chai-paani* (expenses) was taken care of. The owner wisely pretended to agree to their demands and requested for some time to arrange for the money.

'The video and audio recordings documented how this pack of wolves went hunting together and tried to intimidate the common man and extort money from complainants. Thankfully, they were caught accepting the bribe the very next day.'

At that moment, Rekha announced that dinner was ready. All of them headed to the dining room. Ravi ate in silence, processing everything Shekhar had told them so far. Corruption had infected the system like a deadly virus. No department was free from it. The common man had to deal with dishonest officials daily and there was very little help to be had from the system. Shekhar had stood up for them all these years. He struck terror in the hearts of the Bakasurs who misused their power. What was the reason behind his determination to fight corruption? How had he become this relentless crusader and found innovative ways to catch the Bakasurs of our time? Unable to contain his curiosity, he asked, 'Mamaji, what has driven you to fight corruption? Tell us your secret, please.'

With a cryptic smile and a nod, Shekhar said, 'Corruption and pigs.'

'Corruption and pigs? I don't understand, Mamaji,' Pradeep sounded thoroughly confused.

The mysterious smile still intact on his face, Shekhar explained, 'In life, all of us are subjected to certain influences. I've also been exposed to many; some good ones, fortunately.

'When I was young, my semi-literate father drilled into my mind that money made by corrupt means was equal to human excrement. Only pigs would eat it. He always advised me to be happy with my hard-earned money. I'm lucky to be the son of such an upright man. Whatever we learn and imbibe in childhood, we remember all our lives. His message, "corruption and pigs," is so deeply ingrained on my mind that I'll hate dirty money till my last breath. When I see others amassing money by corrupt means, I consider them to be swine.

'When I grew up and started work, my wise senior officer counselled me and asked me to remember two words: "Give justice." If the scales of justice are tilted, you have done an injustice to someone. Only corruption tilts the scales. I simply hung on to those words and as a result, everything fell into place. There was never a question of compromise, come what may. This is why I remain obsessed with the evil of corruption.'

Pradeep was the first to respond. He was full of praise for his uncle. 'Mamaji, a truly rich man is one who is so expensive that no one can afford to buy his character. And that's what you are.' He added with a smile, 'But I also think that you are still a boy at heart.'

Suman scolded him, 'Pradeep, stop your wisecracks. You should learn how to talk to your elders.'

'No, Ma. I didn't mean to offend anyone. Mamaji is the person I admire the most in the world. What I meant to say is that he has the same enthusiasm he must have had when he was a boy. His determination to fight corruption never wanes. That's such a rare quality.'

Suman gave Pradeep a smile and turned to her brother. 'Shekhar, you are a brave crusader,' she said. 'But, let me tell you, whenever we read about your cases in the newspapers or watch news reports about them on TV, I am scared that someone you have exposed may harm you—even physically.'

₹50

Rekha joined in with a complaint, 'Yes. You must talk to him about this. I'm tired of questioning him because whenever I raise the matter, his stock reply is that a person only dies once. May as well live a full life without fear.'

Shekhar smiled. 'I'll stick to that motto. Even when I took action against the dangerous narcotics mafias and other such criminals, nothing happened to me. I never received any threats. When we're legally right, no one dares to touch us. Moreover, everyone knows that I always work for reforming the system. There's no personal motive involved. And what danger do I face from politicians? At the most, they can only try to transfer honest officers. Who cares, really?

'One problem does exist. And I won't deny it. That's the danger posed by tainted bosses who try to spoil our service records, which leads to unwarranted litigation. Luckily, such things have never happened with me so far. Perhaps they're also afraid of me. I've been fortunate to have the complete support of my family. I know I'm blessed that way. Rekha and Abhi always stand by me. That's more than enough.'

As Suman and her sons looked at their smiling faces, Abhi added, 'Of course, we also have our extended family—our pets to give Papa a boost and brighten up our days.'

Shekhar and Rekha were only too happy to agree.

'Shekhar, I've one doubt though. You're so dedicated to your work that you might find life difficult after retirement. What do you say, Rekha?' Suman asked.

'You're right, Suman. But the trouble with retirement is that you never get a day off, isn't that what they say?' Rekha asked with a smile.

'I have to agree,' Shekhar said. 'Rekha has the last word in any argument. I'm afraid anything I say after that will be the beginning of yet another argument.'

Rekha said, 'Am I wrong, Suman? A man should forget his mistakes. It's no use two people remembering the same thing.'

Shekhar laughed and looked at Rekha fondly.

Suman gave the couple a smile and wished them well.

As their mother, uncle and aunt were winding up the conversation, the boys made travel plans for the next day. They decided they would go on a Metro ride and also visit India Gate. Once their plan was in place, they went to bed.

Day Four

Abhi woke up when Bujji began to lick his hand. It was too early to go for a walk. She would have to wait for a while no matter how eager she was to step out. The others were still sleeping and so Abhi got out of bed without making a sound. Bujji followed him out of the room, whimpering.

Later, while the day was turning uncomfortably hot, Shekhar dropped the boys off at the Civil Lines Metro station and reminded Abhi that they should be back in time for lunch. Abhi was aware that Mr Subramaniam's family would join them for lunch that day. Mr Subramaniam was an upright and highly respected IAS officer, who had dealt with many challenges in his career.

'Sure, papa. We'll be home for lunch,' Abhi promised.

At the station, Abhi reached the counter to purchase the tickets for Gurgaon but he changed his mind suddenly. He asked his cousins if they would like to visit AIIMS.

'I'd love to,' said Ravi. Pradeep was also eager to join them.

They boarded the train and found three empty seats. The train chugged along and Abhi told his cousins the story of the family that was coming to lunch that afternoon.

Mr Subramaniam had to handle a lot of problems in his own department. And on the home front, he had to deal with a totally different issue. His children, who were studying in a good school, had been frequently telling him about their rich classmates who gloated about their exclusive cars, mobile phones, late-night birthday parties and expensive gifts. He had advised them often, 'We should never compare ourselves to thoroughly corrupt bureaucrats and dishonest business people.'

When Abhi fell silent, Ravi changed the subject. 'Tell me something,' he said. 'When you finish your medicine course, what would you like to opt for: a government job or the corporate sector?'

'Haven't given it any thought at this stage. Why do you ask?'

'I want to remain totally honest in life. But hearing about Mr Subramaniam and others like him, I have a feeling that it's difficult for honest people to survive in the government sector,' Ravi said.

'I can understand your dilemma, Ravi,' Abhi replied. 'But what I have learnt from papa is that honest people may face certain hardships, but they derive great satisfaction in following the path they choose and the reputation they gain in the process. He says, "The corrupt may say we are insane. But let me tell you, we don't suffer from our insanity. We enjoy every minute of it." As a matter of fact, the opportunities you get to serve people while in government service are many. Seeing how happy and satisfied papa is, I often feel that I should also join the government sector.'

Looking at a well-dressed man who had rushed into their compartment at Chandni Chowk station, he said, 'If earning money is the only goal, one should join the corporate sector of course.'

Pradeep agreed, 'You are absolutely right, Abhi. In the corporate world, people are stressed and depressed but still well-dressed…'

The train sped ahead and the boys gazed out of the window. Abhi said, 'Delhi is the hub of modernization. Look at the widening of roads, the construction of new flyovers and chic malls, the state-of-the art buses and the sea of trendy cars. There are skyscrapers here that can give the ones in Manhattan an inferiority complex.'

Ravi's tone was tinged with irony when he spoke. 'So far, I've been thinking it was the other way round.

It appears that Delhi has still a long way to go before calling itself modern.'

At home, Rekha had changed the menu to a strict vegetarian one to suit the Subramaniams. As she was supervising the lunch preparations, she told Suman about their guests. 'They are very nice people and dear friends,' she said. 'You know, last summer, they faced a serious dilemma. Like every year, the city was sizzling because of the *loo* (hot, dry wind) and the dust. Mr Subramaniam's wife used to tell me that their children stayed at home, spending their time dusting every piece of furniture in the house, while their friends went on holiday to exotic destinations in Europe and other countries.

'They would come back and flaunt the expensive purchases they had made, describe their ice-skating, the dishes they had eaten, the glamorous tourist spots they had visited, the luxurious hotels they had stayed in and so on. The Subramaniams' children did not explicitly say anything. But every time they spoke about their friends, their disappointment was clearly visible. Finally, one day, the Subramaniams shared their concerns with us.'

'What did you do then?' Suman asked.

'Shekhar simply told Mr Subramaniam, "There's

nothing to worry about. This is a problem that any honest man is sure to face. Let's all go to Dehradun and Mussoorie along with our families." We hired a minibus and went to Dehradun and Mussoorie with our friends, the Payengs. The trip was fun. We enjoyed going there as a group. It was also a great relief for both Mr and Mrs Subramaniam.'

Abhi showed them around the premier medical institute—the crowded Trauma Centre and the wards, and further ahead, several specializations. Reading out the names of doctors along with their long list of degrees which were on display, he told his cousins that they were all reputed experts. Pointing at the nameplate of a psychiatrist, Abhi said, 'He's not only a great psychiatrist but he also an interesting conversationalist. He has many stories to tell us. Once he told us about a woman who went to a psychiatrist complaining that she feared that a dangerous creature was hiding under her cot. The doctor assured her that he would cure her of the fear but that it would require at least twenty sessions. When she enquired about his fee, he stated that each session would cost her five hundred rupees. She went back and told her husband about it. When she never came back, the doctor himself called her up to enquire about her decision. She answered, "Thank God, I am now fully cured, doctor. My husband simply arranged to have the legs of our bed cut."'

Pradeep and Ravi guffawed. Abhi then herded them towards the classrooms, laboratories and well-stocked library. Their next stop was the AIIMS canteen, where many senior doctors were freely mingling with their students and juniors. Ravi told them this was a surprise to him. Things were very different at his engineering college where strict hierarchies were maintained on the campus.

After making sure that his cousins had visited every spot worth seeing at AIIMS, Abhi decided it was time to go home. There was no question of keeping their guests waiting. Rekha had already given him a call to remind him about lunch.

As they stepped off the train and were walking out of the station, a young couple, clearly newly married, were ahead of them. They looked thrilled and were holding hands. Seeing their delighted faces, Pradeep could not resist from cracking a joke. He said, 'A man goes to a doctor to ask for some medicine that can ensure him a long life. The doctor asks him to get married. The man asked whether that would help him live longer. The doctor quipped that it would certainly help him to steer clear of such thoughts.'

Abhi and Ravi obliged Pradeep with a smile and got into the waiting car. Abhi the philosopher said, 'Both love and squabbles are a part of married life. Light and dark, tears and smiles—you have to embrace all of it.'

When they reached home, the boys immediately greeted the guests. Mr Subramaniam, with *vibhuti* (sacred ash) smeared on his forehead and a *rudraksha* (dried stonefruit, which is used as prayer beads by Hindus) chain around his neck, looked like a truly devout man who was at peace with himself. He stood up to greet them. His wife, who was wearing a sari in a special style, smiled at them. Ravi knew that this was the 'nivi style' popularized by Raja Ravi Verma in his beautiful paintings.

Lunch was accompanied by casual chit-chat. Pradeep tried to hide his disappointment and stoically finished the meal. He was disappointed about the lack of meat and kebabs, which had gone missing after the menu was changed to strict vegetarian.

After their guests left, the three of them headed out again. Their favourite mode of transport was the Metro. The train took them to India Gate and Connaught Place. They loved the train rides and would not trade it for any other mode of transport. Edward Lutyens' architectural feats in and around Connaught Place fascinated them. The sight of India Gate fuelled them with patriotic fervour. The markets in Janpath charmed them even on that hot day. And the train ride in a comfortably air-conditioned coach cooled them down.

When they were back at home, Pradeep's face flushed with pleasure at dinner when he found non-vegetarian kebabs along with tandoori chicken on the menu. Rekha's specialty—caramel pudding—too made his eyes light up.

Shekhar waited for a while before asking, 'How was your Metro ride? And what sights did you see?'

Putting down the chicken drumstick, which he was chewing on, Ravi said, 'Mamaji, the Metro rides were lovely. The coaches are clean and well maintained. I find it astonishing that the roads are so chaotic while the trains run so smoothly. People overtake each other on the roads, jump lanes, spit, drop litter from cars and buses and show a total lack of discipline and civic sense. Surprisingly, this is not seen in Metro travel. No spitting and jostling, people wait in queues for their turn. What an amazing contrast!'

Shekhar agreed. 'Your observations are spot on. The Delhi Metro has not only eased some of the pressure on road transport and reduced the dependence on the killer blue line buses but also brought a sense of discipline, orderliness as well as cleanliness. I wish that this "Metro-culture" would gradually spread to the roads as well.'

Ravi said, 'Not only in Delhi, Mamaji, it should spread to every place across the country.' When Shekhar nodded, Pradeep jokingly remarked that even the cattle and stray dogs on the roads could do with some discipline and civic sense!

This reminded Ravi of the stray cattle they had seen in a posh area that afternoon. He wondered aloud how they were permitted to roam around in the capital city so freely.

Shekhar smiled. 'Oh, the cattle! No one can catch them. They belong to VIPs including some judges, who keep them in their spacious official bungalows in the posh parts of the city.'

'What?' Suman was astonished. Her kohl-rimmed eyes widened and her eyebrows shot up.

Shekhar understood why she was surprised but there was nothing to be done. Cattle would wander around the streets as long as their owners were in positions of power...He sat on the lawn with the rest of the family, waiting for coffee to be served. The lawn was moist from a fresh round of watering. The grass gleamed. Sitting at a dignified distance, Frooti was watching everyone. Bujji and Bablu were rolling around, scratching their backs and enjoying the feel of the soft grass.

Ravi asked, 'Mamaji, I found CISF men handling security in the Delhi Metro. Is this why discipline is maintained? The local police in general seem to be very rude, uncouth and corrupt.'

Shekhar explained, 'A moot point. See, the local police do play a role in regulation. But you must realize that the culture of the Metro can't be created by them alone. Please remember, when it comes to the police, you should know that there are good and bad apples in the force.'

Ravi understood this fact but he still had doubts. 'Mamaji, instead of misdirecting their energies, why don't the local police try to catch criminals and help in reforming them? Surely there are ways to achieve this. Will it not be a great service to society? Will it also not change their dented image?'

Shekhar gave it some thought. After a pause, he said, 'Perhaps it's the system that is responsible. Although the purpose of punishment is primarily to reform a criminal, unfortunately, it rarely happens since most of the police and prison officials are not inclined to work on it. Let me tell you the stories of Sunil and Lambu so that you know what really happens.'

Thrilled that he had volunteered to tell them the stories this time, instead of them having to prod him to share, they waited for him to speak. Abhi was familiar with these stories. Yet, he hung around to hear them again.

Shekhar started with Sunil's story which had happened right in the heart of Delhi.

'Sunil was fed up with his life of crime. He had committed enough thefts and burglaries for one lifetime. He had been convicted and served his jail term. He knew it was time to make some changes so he could lead a clean life as a decent human being. He began to realize the true value of such a life when he started to run a juice shop in a busy area in the city.

Once, he told me how much he regretted his past life. With the trials of his cases delayed for years and lawyers squeezing out his blood with adjournments, he had to commit more crimes to survive. Had he been convicted in the beginning itself, perhaps he would have ended his life of crime earlier. Anyway, he was leading a life like any other ordinary man now. Yet, he had to report to the police officer at the local station at regular intervals to confirm that he was living in the vicinity and was not indulging in any crime at all. The police also visited him periodically to check his whereabouts.

One day, a new officer, Virender, came to check on him at night. The officer to whom he was reporting earlier had been transferred to another station. Arrogantly, Virender told him, "Hey, I want you to come see me at the police station tomorrow at ten o'clock. Don't forget and don't be late."

"Yes, Sir. I will be there."

The next day, Virender began to bombard him with questions. Sunil humbly stated, "Sir, I've stopped my criminal activities altogether. I'm now a happy man, quietly doing my business and living my new life." His face glowed with pride and happiness.

Virender said, "Ok. But you're still a proclaimed offender as far as the police is concerned, you know. What do you have to say to that?"

"Sir, I am aware that a warrant is pending against me. But it was a false case foisted on me. I never committed any such offence."

Virender gave him a sardonic smile. "Nevertheless, you are a proclaimed offender, remember. Only I can help you conceal this fact."

Sunil felt totally helpless.

With a demonical look, Virender made his demand. "If you want me to do you that favour, you need to take care of my *chai-paani*. And it should be at least fifty thousand rupees every month."

Sunil was flummoxed. "Sir, my business is very small. How can I pay you so much?"

Virender warned him in a threatening tone, "I don't need to concern myself with that. It's your choice. You may pay from your business or you may commit crimes again. But I want that money every month. And if you don't pay, I'll arrest you and hand you over to the police station where you are listed as a proclaimed offender."

Sunil pleaded with him but Virender did not relent. A dejected Sunil burst into tears. Virender gave him an option. "Look, forget your business. I've a friend who is a businessman and has a lot of money. I'll arrange for you to work with him for a good salary. Your task is something special though it's very simple. When the businessman transports a huge sum of cash, say fifty-sixty lakhs or more, any time, you should inform me immediately so that I can depute a gang of thieves to loot him. Again, let me remind you that if you play tricks or fail in the task, you will immediately be behind bars as I warned you earlier."

Sunil realized he had no other option. He agreed to take on the task.

Virender introduced him to Sanjay, his businessman "friend" as Sunil, a dear cousin from his village. Sanjay trusted Virender and hired Sunil to assist him in his business.

In course of time, Sunil took a liking to Sanjay. He detested Virender and decided not to stand by his commitment to Virender. Yet, whenever Virender made enquiries, he gave him some excuse or other to keep him in good humour. He kept his liking for Sanjay to himself.

Meanwhile, a man called Kapoor who was a defaulter of a bank, learned that Virender had a close relationship with the recovery agents of the bank. Together, they had been ensuring that the bank was not paid and instead, they were sharing the money.

One day, Virender had caught a gang of thieves including their leader and cracked a dozen cases of vehicle theft. As some of Virender's colleagues were busy interrogating them, Virender was focused on preparing their dossiers so as to complete the formalities of their arrests. Kapoor came in that day to the station to meet him with a reference in hand.

Virender asked Kapoor to wait for a while. When he had wrapped up his work, he spoke to Kapoor who had waited for an hour to meet him. Kapoor introduced himself and told Virender about the difficulty he was facing in repaying his loan. Virender agreed to help him, provided Kapoor paid him five lakh rupees against his default of ten lakhs. Kapoor was shocked. He protested that the amount was too high and told him that he would have paid the five lakhs to the bank itself had he had that sum with him. They had an argument and tempers rose. Virender's mind began working in overdrive. Kapoor had invited trouble for himself not knowing what kind of man Virender really was.

In the next few minutes everything changed. Virender quickly made a big deal with the gang-leader of the vehicle thefts and let him off. In his place, he framed Kapoor as the main accused in the same cases and nabbed him then and there. Kapoor's protests were ignored. Virender laughed at him. Kapoor realized that it was futile to protest and began thinking of ways to defend himself. Finding that Virender was bragging about the deal he had struck with the gang-leader, he waited for an opportune moment and flicked the dossier of the gang-leader that was lying on Virender's table. Nobody noticed what he had done.

Later, when Kapoor was sent to jail, his young wife visited Virender to ask for help. Swept away by her beauty, he tried to make a pass at her. She ignored his advances. Then he came up with a disgusting proposal—if she agreed to sleep with him, he would help her husband. In tears, the distraught young woman left the police station.

Virender became very nervous that night when information received at the police station revealed that the woman had swallowed several sleeping pills. He rushed from work to his businessman friend, Sanjay, for help. Together they went to the woman's place and ensured that the doctors took good care of her. Finally, when she was declared to be out of danger, Virender went back to the police station, relieved.'

'What a creepy man! Such people should be sacked and also punished severely,' Suman said.

'Yes,' Rekha agreed. 'But Shekhar will tell you how the *rakshas* was protected. He's not the only one, there are many more like him according to Shekhar.'

'After a few days, Kapoor, who was sulking in prison and waiting to take revenge, got out on bail,' Shekhar continued. 'Without wasting time, he used a copy of the dossier he had stolen along with his complaint as proof to allege that Virender had implicated him and that he had let the real culprit off after taking a huge sum of money from him.'

'An enquiry was ordered against Virender. It was now Virender's turn to worry. Apprehensive that raids might be conducted on his house, he hurriedly bundled up the things he had at home—four illegal country-made pistols, some packets of brown sugar and a large quantity of gold. Then he told Sunil to meet him urgently. By this time Sunil's loyalty to Sanjay had cemented. Yet, he had never told Sunil about Virender's evil designs and the deal he had struck with him.

Virender informed Sunil that he wanted to leave a packet with Sanjay for a few days. Noticing the traces of anxiety on his face, Sunil suspected that something was wrong. Anyway, he went along with Virender's plan and headed to Sanjay's place. He opened the packet on the way and managed to sneak a look at the contents. He knew Sanjay would be in trouble if he accepted the packet.

Virender and Sunil reached Sanjay's office. Concealing his anxiety, Virender tried to talk pleasantries with Sanjay for some time. Then, in a casual tone, he told Sanjay to keep the packet with him for a few days. Not suspecting a thing, Sanjay was about to accept it when he saw Sunil, who was standing behind Virender, giving him a signal not to keep it. He was puzzled. He wondered how a cousin of Virender's could be giving him such a signal. He thought about it for a while. Sunil was still signalling. Sanjay refused to keep the packet and gave the excuse that he would be going out of station soon and would be away for a long time.

Perhaps, Virender had eyes on the back of his head to notice Sunil's signals. The very next day, he got Sunil arrested for being a proclaimed offender. Sanjay went to see him in jail. He was shocked when Sunil confessed to everything. He told Sanjay about his life of crime and how he had been planted by Virender in Sanjay's house. Sanjay could not believe what he was hearing and he blacked out.

From then on, Sanjay began to carefully record his conversations with Virender. Scared that Virender would play foul, he also kept video cameras ready in his office.

Virender had his own plans. Soon, he organized raids on Sanjay's office and destroyed everything there. The video cameras installed in Sanjay's office recorded his actions. Thus, on Sanjay's complaint, another vigilance enquiry was started against Virender.

But the sad part was that during the enquiry, the evidence given by Sanjay vanished from the files. And every time he produced some additional evidence, Virender was alerted and he in turn threatened Sanjay. This went on until the enquiry was closed. Kapoor's complaint was also closed eventually. See how the vigilance officers colluded with the delinquent officer? Money talks. Money outshouts everything else.

In the end, the criminal in uniform was helped by his colleagues and his department to become much more powerful. Virender was promoted to inspector. And Sanjay, Sunil and Kapoor were left in the lurch.'

'Was there no remedy?' Suman asked.

Shekhar said, 'Fortunately, my chance intervention and reopening of the vigilance enquiries unearthed the real truth later. Virender was suspended and booked in criminal cases. But in how many instances does it happen? There are numerous such instances where the truth is buried and never surfaces—all because of corruption. What I want to say is that even if a criminal really wants to reform himself/herself the existing systems do not help the person.'

'What a criminal in uniform Virender is!' Ravi exclaimed.

'Absolutely. And I don't know how aware you are of the level of corruption in investigations, arrests, false encounters, etc., which are helmed by such crooks. But it's become a routine affair, a given. I only wish that one day the police force will become a professional agency with pride, and swear by the motto of "service." But it requires will on the part of the policy makers and politicians. And, unfortunately, politicians do not want it because the opposition cannot be browbeaten without using the police force. They also need the support of criminals and the various mafias. Obviously, since an honest and transparent police department would not support such aims, the politicians, and for that matter, any government in power would like the present chaos to continue.'

Shekhar grew quiet. Ravi reminded him that he had not shared Lambu's story with them yet.

'I forgot about it,' Shekhar admitted. 'That happened in Goa.'

He went on, 'One day, a report from a police station mentioned that a criminal called Abdul Sattar, who was simply known as Lambu because of his height, had been arrested. It was shocking news to me since this was the same person, a criminal and a drug addict and later a peddler, whom I had got convicted and tried to reform. I was so confident that he wouldn't take up a life of crime again. But it looked like his jail sentence had not done any good and he had remained the same as before. Lambu was brought into my office. I was miffed when he tried to touch my feet. Though he didn't say a word, I noticed tears trickling down his cheeks. Was it catharsis or helplessness? Or was he shedding crocodile tears?

Lambu pleaded, "Sir, please don't be angry with me. Don't be disappointed either. I can say proudly that I'm a reformed criminal and a decent human being now. Crime is a thing of the past for me in spite of the difficult times I had in jail."

Trying to control his sobs, he said, "I say difficult times because the staff inside are not interested in reforming us. They believe we are criminals and treat us like criminals and want us to remain so. They encourage the formation of gangs. Drugs are smuggled in by them and peddled at a high premium. The foreigners and the rich manage everything they want—liquor, drugs, good food and even women. Jail is a den of corruption; those who attend to the personal chores of the staff and help them make an extra buck are looked after well and spared hard tasks, while the others are bullied and exploited. In a state of frustration, the convicts feel helpless and seek comfort in each other's company and forge alliances for future operations." He paused to wipe his tears.

"But believe me, Sir," he continued. "I withstood the rigours and discrimination inside. I came out and, undeterred by the snide comments from people, started a new life. I set up a small business. After observing my conduct for a few months, society has accepted me. I am living happily with my family. You may conduct any enquiry. You will find that I am telling you the truth."

Then, his face distorted by fear and hatred, he began to tell me about what had happened at the police station.

"Sir, your police force has not been able to catch the gangs operating in the recent spate of robberies and dacoities. Therefore, in order to save their skin, they're simply rounding up innocents. I'm only one such victim." He had to pause because he was furious.

After a moment, he spoke again. "It's not only the arrest that's a matter of concern. As a reformed man, I've other objections. Sir, you were kind to me even when I was a known criminal. But look at your staff. They have no such thoughts or feelings. For them, criminals and police are two classes apart, whose converging point is corruption."

He questioned how there could be reform when policemen resorted to inhuman treatment. He had suffered horribly in police custody.

"They picked me up from my shop and beat me constantly at the police station, asking me to confess to crimes I'd never committed. Then they chained me to an iron cot in the barrack the whole night without food or water. Late in the night, when I was dying of thirst, I asked the sentry for a glass of water. With a cocky grin on his face, he brought a mug of water, and acted as if he would pour it into my mouth. Instead, he unzipped his trousers and urinated in my mouth. I was disgusted and I lost control. Surely, you can imagine my plight. I spat on him and was overcome by the impulse to bite him. He punched my face. The bruise on my face and the swelling on my lips are a result of that blow."

He began to wail loudly. I was speechless. What could I say to console him?'

Suman stared at Shekhar, aghast at the cruelty. Ravi and Pradeep were in shock.

Shekhar continued. 'As he was weeping, the giant six-and-a-half feet Lambu shrunk into a ball and asked me, "Sir, you want reform. But, please tell me what to do. Should I return to crime? My heart is against it, but your system is forcing me back into it."'

'I tried to find the right words. My heart was broken by his plight. He was in an impossible position.'

Pradeep asked, 'Did you take any action against the policeman involved?'

Looking dejected, Shekhar replied, 'I took action against the constable anyway. But I was also angry with the system since no one's really concerned about people like Lambu. Everyone—senior officers and the government—only believes in statistics. Actually, those who lack strategies resort to juggling with statistics to fool society. As a matter of fact, what society needs is not statistics but real change on the ground.'

Ravi asked, 'Can a policeman really behave like this, Mamaji?'

Grimly nodding his head, Shekhar confirmed, 'Unfortunately, it's true. It's been happening all over the country. The sad aspect is that, many times, senior officers not only ignore such incidents but also condone them and protect such people.'

Day Five

Pradeep and Ravi had visited AIIMS, India Gate, Rashtrapati Bhawan and Parliament. Abhi planned to show them other important places in the city as well. He wanted his cousins to see every sight worth seeing while they were staying with him. He made a mental note—he would take them the zoo and Purana Quila (Old Fort). Then, all three of them would go to bustling Chandni Chowk.

Everyone agreed with Rekha when she suggested that they should visit Rajghat first thing in the morning that day. She wanted to make sure the boys visited Rajghat before they headed out for sightseeing. Once they were gone, she would find it hard to get hold of them. And so, early that morning, they drove to Rajghat where dewdrops shone on the sprawling lawns. The melodious notes of hymns filled the quiet. They were joined by morning walkers and a few rare visitors like them who had come to pay their respects to the Mahatma.

Rekha was sure that the visit to Rajghat was an experience the boys would treasure. After they returned, they had a hearty breakfast at home. Then, the boys headed to the zoo and Purana Quila (Old Fort) with Abhi at the helm. After spending a few hours there, they moved on to Chandni Chowk.

In contrast to the gigantic structures at Connaught Place, here, they found only ordinary and old-looking ones that were festooned with many dusty overhead wires. Unlike the majestic Raj Path, there was a labyrinth of narrow lanes here. But there were many famous old shops with boards displaying their vintage. The gullies carried the names of the specialties—jalebiwallahs, paranthawallahs, Karachi Halwawallah, etc. Everything was a landmark and history was a living presence in these lanes.

Abhi led them through the alleys of paranthawallahs where they stopped at a restaurant for lunch. Flustered by the incredible range of paranthas on the menu, they took a while to place their order. Apart from mouthwatering paranthas, they also drank a glass of lassi each. This had to be the most satisfying meal they had had in recent times.

After lunch, they walked down the streets lined with jewellers and cloth merchants. Cycle-rickshaws carrying tourists and smiling foreigners whooshed past them. The lanes were filled with people and the three of them were overwhelmed by the sight of the milling crowd.

Ravi had to raise his voice so they could hear him. He asked, 'What's this place, Abhi? It's terrible. Vehicles, cyclists, pedestrians and hawkers—the lanes are clogged. There's no room here for these rickshaws. Moreover, the pavements meant for pedestrians have been taken over by shopkeepers and vendors. Such a mess!'

Some policemen were patrolling the streets nonchalantly. They looked on as pedestrians were forced to walk on the roads meant for vehicular traffic.

'Perhaps the municipal officials are also indifferent to this state of affairs,' Abhi added.

Pradeep's response was the exact opposite. He said, 'I feel this place looks like a lively festive fair. Look at the rich variety of goods. Where else would you find it? I swear shopping here is a great pleasure.'

Ravi did not bother to contradict him. He did not have the energy for an argument. They roamed around the market picking up various items—T-shirts, kerchiefs, small electrical goods, etc. Pradeep, an expert at haggling, helped the others every time they made a purchase. He got them the best deals and they thanked him for it. They also spent some time in Kamala Nagar afterwards where did they did the rest of their shopping before heading home.

The pets greeted them like long lost friends when they got home. Frooti looked at Pradeep fondly, wagging her tail and barking gleefully.

Ravi was mulling over something he had heard during the day. He decided to ask Shekhar about it. Mamaji would surely be able to clear his confusion.

He said, 'I found people touting several temples in the city as *"pracheen mandir"* (ancient temple) today. Are they saying that the gods in the older temples are more powerful or sanctified than the ones in the new temples?' he asked.

Shekhar praised his sharp thinking and Ravi was delighted by the praise. 'I totally agree with you, Ravi,' Shekhar said. 'God is the same everywhere. This is all about playing with the devout's religiosity and profiting from it.

'Delhi is a contradictory place, you know. Here, people are ready to give *daana* (seeds) to birds but are reluctant to give *daan* (alms) to the poor. You must have seen that people stop their cars at junctions to religiously offer birds and squirrels grains and water, and bread and bananas to monkeys, especially on Tuesday, which is a holy day for Hindus. But the number of people offering grains being many, and birds being too few, there are many leftovers. Urchins go about collecting them to sell them to roadside vendors. They, in turn, get them ground into flour and make cheap snacks, which they hawk in the gullies.'

'What?' Suman looked puzzled. She could not understand the dichotomy. If people went out of their way to feed animals to seek God's blessings, they could make an effort to feed the needy too?

'People who indulge in cheating, fraud, dishonesty and corruption apparently feel insecure and become more religious than others,' Shekhar said. 'In order to fool such people, gurus and astrologers mushroom in every corner promising to find ways for them to wash away their sins. Moreover, cashing in on their sentiments, temples too spring up, prominently displaying the boards, "*Pracheen* Shiv *Mandir*", "*Pracheen* Hanuman *Mandir*", etc., in order to attract such people. They are ready to pay bribes to God in the form of donations. Many people are fooled by the word "*pracheen*" in this "*pracheen*" city.

'If you observe carefully, you'll see that conmen in society are conned by religious conmen. The important question to ask is: who's the bigger conman of them all?'

Everybody laughed. Pradeep suddenly let out a triumphant cry. He had forgotten to tell them about the deal he had struck at Kamala Nagar during his shopping spree.

He proudly said, 'If we're not careful, the vendors here would really fleece us. Initially a vendor quoted a price of three hundred rupees for a packet of a dozen kerchiefs. I used all my best tricks to strike a bargain. I firmly stuck to fifty rupees. He did not budge. Finally, I acted as if I didn't care for the item and pretended that I was leaving. He came running after me and agreed to sell the packet for fifty rupees. You should ask Abhi and Ravi how I haggled!'

Rehkha was very impressed. She asked him to go with her the next time she went shopping. 'Let me see the kerchiefs you bought,' she said, tearing open the packet.

'Why did you purchase such small ones? They can be used only by babies,' Rekha cried out.

Pradeep's face turned pale. 'No way, Mami. I haggled and paid for the very large ones that the vendor showed me.' When Rekha took out the pieces one by one, he was stunned. 'Nooo! These aren't the ones,' he said. 'These aren't even one-fourth the size of the kerchiefs I saw.'

Rekha smiled, 'Oh! It means that you were tricked, my child.'

Pradeep began to curse the vendor. 'Can we go back there and find him?' he asked Abhi.

'No, they never remain at the same place.'

Pradeep looked downcast.

Noticing his drooped shoulders and disappointed look, Shekhar reassured him, 'Pradeep, don't worry. This is a small matter. Everyone gets cheated here one time or the other. In fact, even very experienced people get conned, you know. This is Delhi, remember.'

Rekha too consoled him, 'Your Mamaji is right, Pradeep.' She went on to share an embarrassing incident from her life. She had narrowly missed being cheated by a conman of a dentist at a posh clinic.

Rekha said, 'I'd gone there for a routine dental check-up. But what he told scared me out of my wits. He said that I had very bad teeth; many of them required fillings and some needed root-canal treatment; and my jaw bone required urgent repair. This would cost around twenty-five thousand rupees but he said he would charge me only twenty thousand. Since the doctor sounded very sincere, I believed him. At the same time, I had a flicker of doubt too. When I mentioned it to your Mamaji, he said that we should go to a government hospital for a second opinion. There, the doctors confirmed that only one tooth required a filling. We felt so relieved and got the job done immediately.'

Smiling fondly at Pradeep, she added, 'Believe me, it happens to everybody at Delhi. You don't have to lose heart over the kerchief scam.'

Pradeep smiled at her. He felt better now that he knew even experienced people were tricked by sly scamsters in Delhi.

Ravi began to talk about the chaos they had witnessed at Chandni Chowk that day. 'Mamaji, we found congestion and only congestion at every spot in the market at Chandni Chowk. And it's the same at Kamala Nagar too. The space meant for pedestrians has been usurped by shopkeepers and hawkers. And

Karol Bagh is no different either. How can this be allowed to happen? What exactly do the police do to improve matters?'

Shekhar told him, 'Certainly it's the job of the police and the municipal authorities to regulate them. But if the concerned officials haven't done that, it's clear that there is something fishy going on. This is yet another organized racket operating in Delhi like illegal parking, prostitution, the narcotics trade, gambling, illegal brewing, etc. Such things can't flourish and mafias can't operate unless they have the blessings of the local politicians and authorities. Even at check-posts at the border, bribes are collected in an organized way. Do you know that gangs from adjoining States steal cattle from the city streets right under the noses of the policemen posted at the check-posts?

'Policemen posted there also become pally with three-wheeler riders going to and from Uttar Pradesh to Delhi and liberally allow them to ply on Delhi roads but they harass local transport operators for petty violations. A sting operation exposed this racket and as many as five policemen and their touts who were collecting monthly bribes were caught.'

Pradeep asked, 'Suppose we don't make a spot payment for the traffic challan that is slapped on us. What happens then?'

Shekhar replied, 'It would only get added to the

lakhs of pending ones piled up in the special traffic courts. Or it could be specially disposed of by an *ahlmad* (employee working in goods, civil or criminal courts) of the court.'

'I don't understand what you mean,' Pradeep said.

Shekhar explained patiently, 'The *ahlmads* of the courts take undue advantage of such a huge backlog and collude with agents and defaulters to dispose of as many challans as they can on the sly at half the rates the challan amounted to. They pocket bribes for doing this and get richer by the day.

'Once, we learnt about the alleged link of the in-charge of the court with this fraud. But we couldn't do much until we sought permission from the High Court as it's needed in such matters. We were ordered not to inform the media about it. Such gag orders are issued even when State government officials are accused of corruption. The Chief Vigilance Commissioner himself has issued such gag orders.

'Anyway, we succeeded in nabbing the *ahlmad* and his agent subsequently, though the link with the judge couldn't be proven. I don't understand why gag orders are given in these instances. Why this misplaced sympathy for the corrupt who are caught taking bribes? We're only losing sight of the larger goal here. With the legal process being very slow, I think it's necessary to spread the word about these people's misdeeds so as to teach others a lesson and ensure deterrence.'

Ravi agreed with Shekhar. Where was the sense in keeping silent about corruption?

'What else did you notice during your city tour today?' Shekhar asked the boys.

Remembering the train of cycle rickshaws at Chandni Chowk, Ravi said, 'Mamaji, cycle rickshaws though attractive and exotic attractions for foreigners, are a real problem at Chandni Chowk. They were everywhere in the congested lanes. It's risky for people to walk close to them; accidents may happen. Incidentally, I found that some city agency was towing away a long line of rickshaws, maybe about fifty of them. Will their owners be really taken to task?'

Shekhar told him, 'What you saw was perhaps a special drive by the municipality. But in one of the sting operations conducted not so long ago it came to light that this is only a periodic, meaningless ritual. Once the vehicles reach the pounds where they'll be kept, owners coming forward to pay bribes would be let off easily.'

Happy to have had such an interesting chat with Shekhar, the boys made plans for the evening. They said goodbye to the elders and headed to the magnificent Jama Masjid, which they were very keen to see. From there, they went to Red Fort to watch the spectacular light and sound show. That was indeed a treat! For dinner, they went to the famous eatery, Karim's and ordered biryani.

When they returned home, they found Shekhar, Rekha and Suman lazing around on the lawn. They had had their dinner about half-an-hour ago.

Pradeep told Rekha that he was peckish.

Rekha was surprised. 'Didn't you go to Karim's for dinner?'

Pradeep sheepishly replied, 'We did, Mami. But I got a plate of biryani which only had bones. There was no meat on them. That's why I'm hungry.'

Ruffling Pradeep's hair fondly, Rekha headed to the kitchen to make him an omelette. Pradeep followed her to the kitchen and so did Suman.

The pets came running in and circled around Rekha. Smiling, she reassured them, 'Hang on, I will make one each for you too.' As if understanding her perfectly, they wagged their tails and waited.

Pradeep thanked Rekha for the omelettte and carried his plate and a cup of coffee out to the lawn to join Shekhar, Ravi and Abhi.

Shekhar asked him if he had heard of the parking mafias which were active in several places in Delhi.

'Parking mafias?' Pradeep asked, his eyes widening. 'I've heard you mention the mafias like the ones in Dhanbad which control the mining areas. But I've never heard of parking mafias. What is it that they do?'

'Well,' Shekhar sighed. 'They're doing very well here and are also close friends of the police.'

Pradeep asked in all sincerity, 'Why should they be so close? What do they have in common?'

'You'll understand when I tell you about a case,' Shekhar said. 'This took place at a busy market complex that belongs to the Delhi Development Area (DDA). As you know, when terrorists attacked some crowded market places in Delhi and killed and injured people, government beefed up security and also installed CCTV cameras in market places to keep watch.

'So, like in many other market places, additional pickets and CCTV cameras were set up in this complex also. A monitoring screen was installed in the chamber of the SHO at the nearest police station so he could keep an eye on the market from his office.

'This complex had a notified free-parking zone to be used by shopkeepers and their customers. Things went on smoothly until a new SHO took over. The SHO had a secret meeting with the parking mafia and struck a lucrative deal with them with the help of a few policemen who acted as the middlemen. Once the deal was in place, all of them got together and cemented their friendship by having dinner together.

'And thus, one winter morning, some local goons employed by the parking mafia showed up at the market complex. Some of the corrupt policemen also got there. Quickly, the goons replaced the free-parking board with a paid-parking one. People were puzzled by this sudden move. The policemen confirmed the change. Immediately, the men from the parking mafia began to collect a fee in the name of parking and even issued receipts to those who paid to create a facade of an authorized contract. Some people quietly paid up and accepted their receipts. Others protested. The angry goons roughed them up and told them to pay the fee. Calling for a truce, the policemen cajolled people into paying. From that day onwards, the mafia thrived and their honeymoon with the police continued for months till the mafia decided to double the charges one fine day.

'They doubled the parking fee without warning. This took many people by surprise but one shopkeeper mustered the courage to oppose it tooth and nail. The angry goons abused him. When he refused to back off, they thrashed him in front of a crowd. The police looked the other way. The distraught man was determined to fight back. He made many enquiries and also filed an RTI application to procure details. He came to know that this was a fraud happening right under the nose of the local police, some of whom were directly involved in it. Garnering support from other aggrieved people like him he made a formal complaint to the police.

'The SHO gave him a strange look when he met him. Then, strongly defending the hike in the charges, he asked, "Why are you so agitated? When

PAID PARKING

the authorities decide something there is a reason for it. You have no option but to pay the fee." He went on to threaten the man, "If the contractor makes a complaint against you for not paying, I will have to take action." When the delegation which had accompanied the shopkeeper complained against the fraud, he furiously denied it was a fraud. Seeing his reluctance to take any legal action against the mafia, the delegation was sure the whole thing was going on with his blessings. They approached the DDA next. Luckily, some of the officers there stood up for them and sent an official complaint to the SHO asking him to stop the illegal operation of the mafia since the DDA had not awarded any contract to them.

'The SHO quickly changed his stand and responded to the DDA by categorically replying that no parking fee was being collected by any contractor and denying every single allegation levelled against them.'

'How could he do that when people were being issued receipts?' Ravi asked.

'Obviously, he was doing this because of the hefty monthly payments the mafia made to him without fail,' Shekhar said.

He continued, 'Frustrated, the complainants took their complaint to the vigilance unit of the police. And a sting operation was planned. Soon, spy cameras began to capture evidence. The contractor and his men were seen collecting fees for parking. The paid-parking board and the receipts issued showed up clearly on camera. The beat policemen were found comfortably mingling with the contractor and his men. They were also seen demanding bribes from people who wanted to pitch a tent for a sale on a Sunday in the parking area. Patrolling policemen were heard talking about the lucrative deals that beat policemen had stuck with the parking mafia. Spy cameras recorded the beat police collecting *haftas* from squatters and vendors saying that they would pass on the money to the SHO.

'With the massive fraud unearthed, and confident that the evidence captured and collected was solid, the vigilance unit shared an exhaustive report with the Commissioner of Police, recommending strong action be taken against the SHO, the beat staff and the contractor at once.'

'Then what happened?' Pradeep asked impatiently.

Shekhar said, 'Jubilantly, the vigilance officers entered the chamber of the Commissioner of Police, not knowing that they were in for a rude shock. The Commissioner looked cool and unflappable and greeted them with a polite smile. In fact, he was a changed man since the time he had learnt to rein in his temper by religiously practising the *Om Shanti* mantra of the Brahma Kumaris.

'Patiently, the Commissioner began to hear the detailed case the vigilance officer who prepared the report presented. Despite his best efforts, he began to lose his composure. He started to ask them questions in an angry tone. His calm expression changed to one of petulance and exasperation. As the vigilance officer went on explaining, the Commissioner's eyes became bloodshot and he stared at the officer as if he had done the wrong thing. And by the time the officer finished speaking, the Commissioner turned aggressive. Not making any effort to hide his annoyance, he asked why the sting operation had been conducted in the first place without his knowledge.

'He would not buy the argument that this was the only way collusion in corruption could have been exposed. He was in no mood to listen to reason. Furious, he expressed his displeasure at the vigilance unit. A few other officers who had walked into the chamber to discuss a different matter quietly turned back and left seeing the Commissioner so worked up. The *Om Shanti* mantra had failed to work this time.

'Slowly, he made an effort to compose himself. Closing his eyes, he contemplated for a minute, still shaking his head at the audacity of his vigilance officers. The officers watching him were flummoxed. Finally, he opened his eyes. Pummelling the table with his fist, he announced his decision, "You'll stop sting operations forthwith. This is a direct order."

The officers were flabbergasted by the reprimand they were given for conducting such a meticulous operation. They left the room without a murmur.'

Ravi was shocked to hear this. 'Why did the Commissioner favour that rotten SHO?' he asked.

Shekhar replied, 'The SHO was posted there by that Commissioner. You may surmise the rest of the reasons. Corruption is such a pervasive influence. It's immune to the tenets of the Art of Living and the *Om Shanti* mantra.

Pradeep said, 'When money talks, no one bothers to check the grammar.'

Ravi wondered aloud, 'Why is it that money corrupts even the sanest heads?'

Shekhar replied, 'Wonderful, my boys! How come you have become so brave and outspoken after spending only four days in Delhi? Makes me think this is a great place to learn life lessons. Nowhere else will you find such a wealth of insights.'

The boys took Shekhar's observation with a pinch of salt. But they were happy to be called brave and outspoken by their crusader uncle who struck terror in the hearts of the Bakasurs who were looting the country.

'What happened to the people who complained against the SHO and the parking mafia, Mamaji?' Ravi asked.

Shekhar replied, 'The aggrieved people who had worked so hard to collect evidence did not relent though they were upset. The shopkeeper could not forget how he had been roughed up in full public view. They stood together and moved the High Court. When he came to know of it, the Commissioner acted at once! Even before the matter came up before the court, a case was registered and the SHO was shifted out. The High Court was informed and the matter was disposed of without further delay. The wrath of the High Court was thus dodged. Later, the investigation of the case was quietly handed over to a pliable officer.

'But in course of time, the poor complainants began to be harassed on some flimsy pretext or the other. A punishment for complaining against police officers! How dare anyone complain against the police even if they were neck-deep in corruption?'

Ravi said, 'Mamaji, in rural areas, I can understand the police being all-powerful. But, in Delhi, it is beyond belief that this goes on. Everyone expects Delhi to be the role model for the rest of the country.'

'Ravi, if people are wise, they'll choose sincere leaders as their rulers. A strong and independent Lokpal and Lokayuktas would then certainly become a reality and things would surely change for the better. If corruption in high places is tackled systematically and sternly, it becomes very easy to handle the corruption of the lower functionaries. It's just like in a war, you know. If the general is attacked, the foot soldiers would run helter-skelter.'

Ravi looked at Abhi and Pradeep. They were about to doze off. But sleep was beyond his reach. He searched desperately for a solution to an extremely serious problem.

Shekhar's phone rang at that moment and he answered the call at the first ring.

Bablu was prancing around on the lawn. Bujji also began running around excitedly. Frooti looked on, disdainful of their childish behaviour. Noticing her watching him, Bujji settled down at Shekhar's feet.

'Look how puny Frooti has disciplined Bujji. It seems like she's taught Bujji to be respectful to elders,' Pradeep sounded surprised.

Shekhar had finished his call. He put away his phone and said, 'When we find so much discipline in the animal world, I don't understand why we are not able to establish any controls in human society.

'Discipline in the animal world is an admirable trait. Look, no animal craves food unless it is hungry. The bigger animals do not go for the kill once their stomachs are full. Nature provides them with the sex drive only for procreation. Dogs mate only when they are in heat. But look at human beings. We like to keep eating whether we're hungry or not. Some people arouse themselves with artificial means in order to have sex. And when it comes to the greed for wealth, what can be said! Instances of rape, sexual assault and corruption are glaring examples of our base cravings. Animals abide by a certain discipline but our controls fail constantly. In that sense, we are worse than animals.'

Ravi wondered if there was any hope on the horizon. Shekhar had shared so many instances of crime and corruption. The system seemed to be failing at multiple levels. He asked Shekhar, 'The system is broken and it's unable to reform criminals. Do you think that crime will go on increasing or will there be some respite? Is there any way to control it and bring about a total overhaul?'

Shekhar took his time to come up with an answer. There was no easy way out of this mess and no readymade solutions on offer.

He said, 'Well, people rightly make a noise when crime is on the rise. When the population count rises and economic activity increases; when there's incessant migration to cities; when there's economic deprivation and the gap between the poor and the rich widens dramatically, crime is bound to increase.'

'So, what's the way out, Mamaji?' Ravi asked anxiously.

Shekhar explained, 'Primarily, only ethics, values and discipline can shape a person's character and prevent crimes. Family, society and religion are expected to look after the aspects of ethics and values and the criminal justice system has to take care of the discipline part through punishment and reformation.'

Pradeep wisely pointed out, 'One should know the value of things, not the price. While many parents are ignorant and others are preoccupied with their own professional concerns, who will educate children about the fundamentals of life? Once they miss this chance and children grow up, it'll be too late to teach them the difference between right and wrong.'

Rekha was quick to respond. 'Not every family is unaware of this crucial fact. In our family, we do pay attention to children's ethics and values. We also know the Subramaniams do it and so do the Payengs. There are many others like them.'

'No, Rekha,' Shekhar sounded a note of caution. 'We don't form even a small minority. We're too few in number to make a difference. Pradeep's right to be worried about where society is headed.'

Ravi was of the opinion that schools were simply feeding young people information required to do well in their exams. Inculcating values had unfortunately taken a back seat.

'The old are ruling the country and the young are too busy with social media and online platforms. Where's the time for peer groups to discuss ethics and values? Children are glued to their computers and phones and hardly ever talk to their parents and elders. Neighbours, especially in the big cities, don't socialize with each other because everyone's too busy watching TV,' Pradeep lamented.

'You're right. Do you have any views on the influence of religion regarding this aspect?' Shekhar looked at Abhi for a response.

Abhi was flustered but he came up with an answer in a few moments. 'As far as I understand, religion and God are the same for everyone—both for criminals and the common man. When criminals pray to earn huge amounts of money from their crimes, businessmen and Bakasurs seek God's blessings to amass wealth through wrong means and religious gurus patronize such people, seating them prominently in the front row when they give sermons. I don't think religion is capable of moulding their character. Today's gurus and god-men are satisfied with rituals alone and have no intention of getting rid of their devotees' traits of criminality. In my view, we can't bank on religion to check crime.'

Shekhar summed it up for them. 'This means that all three—family, society, and religion—are not able to check crime. Then the only option left is the criminal justice system, which is made up of the police, advocates, prosecutors, judges and prison officials. As a police officer, I can tell you that favouring the rich and the powerful, victimizing the poor and indulging in corrupt activities have become the hallmark of many a policeman. Even if some of them conduct honest investigations, every case can't reach the courts for trial as adequate evidence is not

available. So, only a few go to trial. Do you think advocates and prosecutors are playing their part well?' Shekhar asked, fixing his gaze on Ravi.

Ravi replied, 'We hear of trials and convictions and also about numerous instances of miscarriage of justice. But, Mamaji, I'm always puzzled when lawyers talk about winning or losing a case. Win or lose, a lawyer's primary role is to bring out the truth, isn't it?'

Shekhar agreed. 'No doubt about that. But unfortunately, the rich and the powerful engage the best legal brains while an average State prosecutor speaks on behalf of the victim and the police. The disparity between them being glaringly obvious, the accused almost always gets relief on technical grounds. Lies are whitewashed and paraded as truths. Witnesses are intimidated or bribed to keep quiet. And facts unfortunately get buried. Thus, even when evil wins over good, they celebrate it as a victory. And the victim, in turn, gets even more victimized. This is the real tragedy of our time.'

Pradeep said, 'True, Mamaji, so many lawyers specialize in turning facts upside down. It seems like that's their only aim. Justice isn't their concern.'

He shared a joke to illustrate his point. 'Seeing a tombstone that said, "Here lies a lawyer and an honest man," a boy asked his father whether there were two people in that grave.'

The others laughed.

Pradeep asked them why judges prefer to keep quiet when they are aware of how lawyers behave. Didn't they have a duty to intervene and set things right? Their inaction was unpardonable.

'There are many upright judges who try to bring out the truth in spite of all the limitations of the system. But the problem is that some are carried away by the spell of star lawyers and acquit the accused. And some judges who even collude with the accused party in order to line their pockets,' Shekhar said. He turned to his sister. 'Suman, do you remember how papa used to speak out against his corrupt fellow judges? I've heard many stories from him.'

Suman said, 'Yes, of course. How can I forget! The values we've inherited are his legacy. He was an extraordinary man and an exemplary judge.'

Shekhar continued to analyze the judicial system. 'One of the hurdles on the path of the prevention of crime is repeated adjournments and judicial delays, which have become a common practice.'

'Why do you say that?' the boys chorused.

'Unless the trial is held immediately, the truth upheld and the accused punished, who will fear the legal process? You must have read about a man of seventy-six whose conviction in a rape case was upheld by the Supreme Court recently. Do you know that this was for an offence he committed over twenty years ago? In what way was this justice? How can it serve as a deterrent for others? In this case, think of the victim. She had borne severe trauma—at the time of the rape and also during the trial. The accused was enjoying his life for years after he was freed on bail whereas she had been enduring a living death, saddled with the stigma of rape,' Shekhar said.

Rekha said, 'Punishment for rape should be so harsh that no one will dare to even think of committing it. Even the law concerning juveniles has to change. Otherwise, rape and other such horrific crimes will go on unabated.'

Suman agreed with Rekha. 'Rape survivors must be treated with much more sensitivity. And rapists should be given the maximum punishment.'

'True,' Pradeep said. 'Survivors shouldn't be treated this way. Unless radical changes are made in our legal process, the callous system leaves them with no option but to suffer.'

'Now, let's talk about prisons,' Shekhar continued. 'The purpose of punishment is retribution but it should be reformation instead. Only then will the situation improve in a meaningful way.'

'We know what happens inside jails because you told us Lambu's story,' Pradeep said. 'Prisons act only as graduation centres of criminal activity. Moreover, we keep hearing that rich criminals and Bakasurs enjoy special privileges behind bars with the help of conniving officials.'

'You've hit the nail on the head. This why the crime rate is on the rise,' Shekhar sighed.

Ravi went to bed that night still searching for an answer. What was the way out? Was the road ahead paved with hope or was the future nothing but bleak?

Day Six

The next morning, by the time they woke up, Shekhar had already left the house. Leisurely, the three boys had a bath and got dressed. When they sat down for breakfast, Abhi shared his plans for the day with them—they could go to Qutub Minar, do a bit of shopping at Mehrauli, have their lunch at one of his favourite restaurants in Green Park and then go watch a movie.

'Hope we can take the Metro this time too,' Pradeep said eagerly.

'Sure, let's,' Abhi said. 'Mehrauli, where the Qutub is located, is quite a long way off.'

Pradeep was delighted. If it was up to him, he would take the Metro everywhere. The train ride was without a doubt the highlight of this holiday as far as he was concerned.

The Qutub Minar was a stunning sight. The seventy-three-metre-high victory tower of Qutb-ud-din-Aibak, built in the early thirteenth century, was an imposing structure. The brothers had read about it in their textbooks but they had not grasped its scale till they actually stood beside it. Feeling dwarfed and humbled by its majesty, they listened to a guide talking about how the structure had a fascinating history. The guide's narration and the ambience of the well-maintained ruins magically transported them to the past through the portals of history.

As they moved on to Mehrauli market for a bit of shopping, Abhi mentioned the farm houses nearby. Shekhar had told him more than once that corrupt money was invested in all these sprawling houses.

Their next stop was Green Park where they walked into a restaurant for lunch and plopped down on the cozy chairs at a table next to the window.

The restaurant was full so a waiter took some time to attend to them. While they were waiting to place their orders, Abhi shared a joke which he had heard at college. He said, 'After examining a patient minutely, a doctor said, "I'm not exactly sure of the cause. I think the reason could be alcohol." Taken aback, the patient said, "That's ok, doctor. I'll come back when you're sober."'

A waiter came to their table as they were laughing at Abhi's joke. Abhi picked up the menu card and found the words 'Green Park' printed in bold at the bottom of it. He smiled as if it reminded him of something amusing.

'Why the smile?' Pradeep asked.

Abhi said, 'Ah! Green Park always reminds me of a corrupt Motor Licensing Officer (MLO) and his Indrabhawan.'

'Indrabhawan? What's that?' Ravi asked.

'Do you remember the licensing fraud of the transport department that I mentioned? When it was busted and the MLO was arrested, his house at Green Park was searched. Though his rank was only equivalent to that of a police inspector, the search team was stunned to see the lavishness with which he had set up his house. It was an ultra-luxurious place and the search team couldn't believe their eyes. Some of the team members must have even felt jealous of the MLO.

'Green Park is considered one of the most expensive locations in Delhi. One needs a minimum of a crore to own even a small flat here. And the MLO had managed to buy a flat in a posh housing society in the area.

'To say that it was merely a flat would be an insult. It was a palace, an entire floor of about 5,000 sq ft. And the interior resembled Indrabhawan as a journalist reported later. Every inch of it including the tiles on the floor was furnished with expensive, new imported items. Every piece of furniture was imported. All the rooms were fitted with split air-conditioners. The search team was bemused to see similar air-conditioners in every bathroom as well. The photographs on display in the house showed the MLO's daughter wearing many costly items of jewellery. In one, she wore a beautiful diamond tiara on her head as if she was a princess. Just imagine, when so much wealth was on open display, how much more could have been kept concealed in the form of jewellery, cash or investments in other assets?

'At that time, it was big news. The story was in the news for weeks. TV channels kept broadcasting it. People in our college canteen talked about it all the time. We also heard some senior doctors teasing each other about their own Indrabhawans.'

'Incredible!' Ravi exclaimed, as the waiter brought them their lunch and set the scrumptious dishes down on their table.

When they reached home in the evening, a visibly excited Bujji came running to the lawn and jumped on them. Frooti waited at a distance, patiently striking her famous penguin posture. She gazed at them with her bright, brown eyes. Bablu was leaping in the air to attract their attention. Pradeep picked him up to play with him.

'Hi, Mami and Mummy! What did both of you do today?' Pradeep enquired.

Suman said, 'We've just got home after shopping at Kamala Nagar. Your Mami took me to some shops where the prices were fixed. No haggling. That way, there's no question of regretting that we could have got a better bargain. By the way, how was your trip?'

'It was wonderful, Mummy. You *have* to see the Qutub.'

'Don't worry. We're going there with Mrs Subramaniam tomorrow.'

Rekha brought them a bowl of boiled corns to munch on while waiting for Shekhar to come home. They watched TV for some time.

Shekhar walked in when it was almost dinner time. After acknowledging the affectionate greeting of their pets, he freshened up. Dinner was served in a few minutes.

'How was your outing today?' Shekhar asked his nephews.

'We went on a long ride to Mehrauli, saw the Qutub Minar and had lunch at Green Park,' replied Pradeep.

'Wow! You must have enjoyed it thoroughly.'

'Yes, Mamaji. Abhi told us about the farm houses around Mehrauli. We also heard about the Indrabhawan of the MLO in Green Park that you had stumbled on,' Ravi said.

With a broad smile, Shekhar told them, 'We could catch only one MLO at that time, you know. My hunch is that every MLO must have such palatial houses and farm houses. They're so rich. Just like the engineers here.'

Ravi suddenly asked, 'Mamaji, where do Aroras hail from?'

'Why do you ask?'

'There are some Aroras in Bhopal who run business establishments. I also saw a shop with their name on it at Mehrauli today.'

'Aroras are mostly businesspeople from Punjab. Incidentally, the name reminds me of the case of an old couple whose property was almost grabbed by the land mafia.'

The boys wanted to hear the story at once.

'It's a long tale. I'll tell you some other time. I'm tired.'

'No, Mamaji. Now, please,' begged Pradeep.

Shekhar gave in to their demand. 'The exorbitant prices of land in Delhi offer an open invitation to many land-grabbing syndicates to become active. This is a very lucrative business which they run without any checks. And they have the support of the police and other government officials. Mafias, working along with such officials, encroach on government land with the hope of grabbing it in a final play. Even private properties are not safe. Aroras are one of the victims.

Twenty-five years ago, land in Delhi was not as expensive as it is today. In those days, a Mr Arora bought a property—an independent house, investing three lakhs of his hard-earned money. He and his family settled down there happily. It may now be worth over five crores.

One day, a year ago, a shabby-looking woman arrived at their house along with some hired muscle, who appeared to be local goons, and a policeman. Dismayed by the intrusion, the Aroras asked them why they had come. Nonchalantly, the woman said, "I have purchased this property. You must vacate it immediately." Mr Arora told her that they had not sold it to her or anybody else.

She replied, "You're not the owner. I have bought it from the original owner. You must vacate it without making any fuss." Her goons were keen to throw the belongings of the Aroras out of the house and get the job done. The Aroras couldn't understand what had happened and asked the policeman, "Sir, we are the owners and we haven't sold it to anyone. How can this woman claim that she has purchased our house from the original owner?"

The policeman glibly replied, "Look, the widow of the original owner has given a complaint to us that you cheated them when you purchased it by not paying the agreed amount. A case has been registered against your family. You stand accused now."

Mr Arora pleaded with him, "A criminal case against us? Sir, we paid all the dues to the husband of the widow before he passed away and got the property duly registered in our name. Where's the question of cheating?" The policeman angrily retorted, "No. We have all the documents. You cheated the old man." Then, looking at the dumbfounded Aroras, he ordered, "The old lady has sold it to this woman and you have no choice. Now, you have to vacate the house."

The Aroras were bewildered. Mrs Arora began to cry.'

Ravi asked, 'Mamaji, it's clear that the deal at the time of purchase was between the Aroras and the old man who was the owner. He's dead. Now, how can the police register a case after twenty-five years merely based on the complaint of the widow?'

'That's the crux of the issue. The police readily registered a case of cheating against the Aroras based on false information and fabricated documents without bothering to check up on the facts with Mr Arora,' Shekhar said.

He continued, 'With this, the real ordeal began for the poor Aroras. They requested policeman to give them some time to resolve the matter. Reluctantly, he agreed. Then they rushed to the court to seek anticipatory bail. They failed. The lower court refused to intervene. Not losing hope, they went to the High

Court and it paid off. An interim stay was granted on their arrests. Though they had received a breather, they were still totally shaken. With the help of some references, they finally made contact with the vigilance unit and poured out their woes.

'Fortune favours the brave and it favoured them again. Their complaint was handled by an officer with a conscience and he made every effort to unravel the tangle. The officer looked into the documents of the Aroras—their sale deed, the payment receipts, the possession record and electricity, water and house tax bills. Everything was genuine. He couldn't find the reason for why a case of cheating had been registered after all these years. He strongly suspected foul play and a conspiracy.

'He also found out some startling facts. The shabby-looking woman had purportedly paid forty-five lakhs for the purchase when she was working as a servant with the widow and was living in a slum. She made the astonishing claim that she had obtained an interest-free loan from someone. When he looked into it, he found out that that person was in no way related to her nor did he strike any business deal with her. He refused to believe that the police hadn't verified her credentials before registering the case against the Aroras. He was sure this was the work of some land-grabbers and the police were also party to it. He submitted a definitive report on the matter.

'The report reached the Commissioner of Police. Good fortune deserted the Aroras this time. He didn't give any relief to them and their struggle continued. They had to fight a long and costly legal battle to prove that the police had framed them.

'See, for no fault of their own, they had to endure the trauma of a potential arrest and live with the fear of losing their hard-earned asset. It was only their tenacity that saw them through those difficult times.'

Sighing deeply, Shekhar added, 'Perhaps, they will still have to do the rounds of the courts if they want to see that action is taken against the errant officers since there has been no such move on the part of the department so far.'

Ravi exclaimed, 'My goodness, policemen can be real criminals! It will be a great service to the nation if one can put an end to their services.'

Shekhar corrected him. 'But that's not the solution. There are many sincere police officers who work hard. Likewise, in other government departments too there are good people as well as some monsters. The real solution lies in taking away the vigilance units from the heads of departments and placing them under the control of independent agencies like Lokpal or Lokayuktas. Even the CBI and anti-corruption units also should be under the control of these agencies if one wants the best results.'

Ravi brought up the matter that had remained

inconclusive the previous night. He said, 'Mamaji, after we talked last night, I thought long and hard about a solution. But to tell you the truth, I couldn't find one. I've failed miserably. For me, the situation looks hopeless especially when, as you rightly said, family, society, religion and even the criminal justice system have lost control over the aspect of crime. What's the alternative then?'

Shekhar was moved by Ravi's youthful sincerity. 'It's a Herculean task since it involves the whole of society,' he said. 'Although people have been coming up with several ideas and options, so far nothing concrete has emerged. I'm glad that you are giving it some serious thought though.'

'But what ideas do you have?' Ravi persisted.

Shekhar said, 'I'd like to take a leaf from the past and learn useful lessons from other places. You know, in the olden days, justice was prompt and effective in panchayats and in the courts of zamindars and kings. Even today, village councils like the kebangs in places like Arunachal Pradesh in the Northeast play a big role in controlling crime. Following their traditional law and procedures, the councils decide disputes absolutely fairly and promptly through consensus and then impose fines.'

Rekha added, 'While we were in Arunachal, we happened to witness their proceedings at a couple of places. They were all wearing their traditional dress and settled down to discuss the dispute. In the end, when they announced the punishment, they also pronounced that the accused would be ostracized by their society and would not be included in any religious rites. We found the man in the dock totally humiliated and dejected. We were told that more than anything else, he was afraid that if he didn't participate in religious rites, his soul wouldn't reach the land of their ancestors. Obviously, everyone was afraid to commit crimes there.'

'It's like the khap panchayats, isn't it?' Suman asked.

'No, not at all. In khap panchayats, even murder is abetted in the name of narrow concepts like caste and *gotra* (clan). In the hills, their classless and casteless society is too mature and broadminded to abet such things. I like them because their interest is only to curb crime,' Shekhar said.

'Now, look at the contrast. We, in the plains, claim to be more civilized than them and have countless laws and procedures. At the same time, there are too many stake-holders here who focus only on serving their own interests. Everyone strives for theoretical and absolute justice. But to what end? We forget the interest of the victim for whom the system exists. We lose sight of the main goal—prevention of crime. What we actually need is a satisfactory judgement and for it to be delivered promptly for both retribution and deterrence to be set in motion. If that happens, crime can be controlled.'

Ravi asked, 'Mamaji, how exactly would you want to use these concepts?'

Shekhar shared some of his ideas. 'Suppose the local bodies like panchayats, mohalla sabhas, etc., are vested with the required authority to dispose of all petty cases and disputes. Under proper guidelines and checks by the supervisory courts, they will be able to deliver prompt and satisfactory judgments. This way, society can also assume some responsibility and gain control over crime. Can you imagine how many such bodies will come into existence? There will be lakhs of them. If this is done, the burden on the regular courts would be eased to an enormous extent. They can do real justice to all the pressing cases in hand without further delay.'

'What about the Bakasurs?' asked Ravi.

'Speedy justice through special courts and extreme vigilance by Lokpal and Lokayuktas would certainly bring about a great difference in controlling them. Here's one more idea. Even at the cost of being called a radical, I'd say that there should be a legal provision for every public authority to undergo periodical lie-detector and narco-analysis tests that are limited to proving their honesty. Surely, it would work as a strong deterrent. Corrupt people may argue that it goes against the Constitution. But, tell me, which

Constitution has permitted them to loot the country? I'm sure that every honest person would volunteer to undergo these tests. Only the dishonest would oppose it.'

'What about the people who cheat in the name of business or industry? Are they also Bakasurs?' Pradeep wondered aloud.

'Why not?' Shekhar asked. 'Cheating is also a serious crime. The formula is simple. Whoever commits a small crime is the devil. One who commits serious crimes is a *rakshas*. And whoever indulges in serious crimes because of greed is a Bakasur. All of them have to be stopped.'

Shekhar's words soothed Ravi's frayed nerves. He announced, 'Mamaji, I've been your admirer for long. Now, thanks to our conversations, I admire you even more. Your thoughts are always about society and the betterment of the country.'

Feeling awkward about his nephew's adulation, Shekhar said, 'I'm only a simple officer, Ravi. Don't praise me to the skies. All I'm saying is that radical changes are required in every department and even in governance.'

'No doubt,' Ravi said.

'Presently, we rely on statistics to assess the performance of a department—like the number of challans issued by the Traffic Unit for example,' Shekhar said. 'But the real yardstick of performance of the Unit should be the public perception of the traffic system—whether it is running smoothly or mired in chaos. Likewise, for every system of governance, there should be a proper index to assess performance. It could be the Public Perception Index (PPI) that is an aggregate of several important factors. Of course, debates and deliberations by intellectuals and experts are needed to arrive at a consensus about such factors. Statistics can only be one of the factors but not the deciding metric.

'Once we arrive at the PPI, reliance only on statistics would be a thing of the past. For instance, even if a single challan is not issued by the Traffic Unit but the system is working well as per the PPI, then, full credit should go to the Unit.'

Ravi hesitantly replied, 'Mamaji, I understand what you're saying. At the same time, I have some concerns and reservations. Will these things ever happen?'

Shekhar was noncommittal. 'That, I can't assure you. I can only give you hope since we live in a democracy and we have the liberty to hope for better.'

Pradeep asked, 'Mamaji, do we have real democracy in our nation? Can we actually accept and experiment with your ideas?'

Shekhar responded, 'You have now brought up the crucial issue. What's democracy when elections are not held as per the will of the people but are stage-managed by the dynasties in power and political leaders? The recent statement of a senior politician in Maharashtra that he had to spend eight crores in an election only confirms an open secret that has been around for years. Even MP posts are said to be sold by political parties for as much as a hundred crore each. Recently, the State Election Commission of Delhi found a serious case of fraud. Thirteen lakh bogus voters and 80,000 who were dead still continue as voters. We are a long way away from being a real democracy. That's why the people's demand for a strong Lokpal has been put on the backburner.' He added, 'I'm very happy that you have begun thinking along these lines though. The future of this country is in the hands of youngsters like you.'

Ravi said, 'Mamaji, you can trust me. You have a powerful influence on me. I promise I'll bring about a change in the thinking of my peers at my college. We'll hold debates and thrash things out. All of us will take a vow to remain honest.'

Smiling at his nephew, Shekhar said, 'I know, Ravi. You're capable of it.'

Peeved, Pradeep jumped in, 'Mamaji, you seem to be underestimating my capability.'

Shekhar said, 'Not at all, my boy. You're no less. But if you can team up you can do wonders.'

'Mamaji, Ravi may lose hope sometimes but I won't,' Pradeep promised. 'It depends on how we see it—we can look at it as a hopeless end or endless hope.'

Shekhar smiled at his nephew and praised his evergreen optimism. He said a cheery goodnight to them and headed to his room.

The boys too settled down for the night after making sure the pets were comfortable on the sofas. They were tired but not sleepy. Pradeep said, 'I think dogs are the best and most loyal pets. They are so affectionate. If you take care of them, they are really grateful for your kindness and love. Unlike cats who act as if they are gods or callous political masters who deserve to be taken care of no matter what they do.'

Abhi smiled at the contrast, which he thought was true.

Ravi said, 'I saw a few Chinkis in Mehrauli market today. There must be many in Delhi. In our college too, there are a couple of them.'

Abhi nudged him. 'Shh...' he warned. 'Never use the word "Chinki" in front of papa. He hates such nicknames.'

Ravi was startled. 'Why?' he asked. 'Even in our college everyone refers to them as Chinkis.'

Abhi chided him. 'Don't you realize that they are only like us except that they have Mongoloid features? Our friends, the Payengs, who are from the Northeast, are simple, frank and plain-speaking people. Even their food habits are simple—they prefer boiled stuff, to which they add ginger and bamboo shoots for taste and flavour. They don't deserve to be called any derogatory names. Please stop using that word…'

Ravi apologized for his mistake. He had never given it serious thought before.

Abhi told him, 'Unfortunately for the students from the Northeast who come here have to put up with verbal harassment in public places when they travel in the city. It's a shame that many people in Delhi view people from the Northeast with suspicion and taunt them about their skin colour and appearance.'

Ravi was thoroughly ashamed of his mistake. Finding him genuinely apologetic, Abhi consoled him, 'It's ok. It happens when we're not aware of the facts. I'm sure you'll never repeat it.'

Day Seven

In the morning, when they returned from a walk, Ravi felt happy that at least the garbage had been cleared away even if the whiff of its stench still floated around. Although it was a sultry day, his pleasant mood stayed intact when they left the house at ten o'clock. As they travelled around town, the cool interior of the Metro kept him happy. He chatted with his brother and Abhi on the way.

By the time they reached Saket District Centre, the weather turned cooler.

'Today, we'll surely have the first rain of the season. Let's rush in,' Abhi tried to hurry them up. Pradeep stood still for a while, staring at the giant shopping malls around—Select City Mall, DLF Place, MGF Mall…

'We'll need at least two days just to walk around these malls. For shopping, we'll need more,' Abhi smiled. 'Maybe when you come to Delhi next time, we'll spend all our time in these malls, ok? Let's get moving now.'

It was like a different world in there altogether. The boys were dazzled by the opulence and the range of goods and branded clothes on display. People were shopping without a care and picking up expensive items. Tempted by a shirt on display in the window when they passed by a Zodiac shop, Pradeep paused. But he was taken aback when he saw the price-tag—three thousand rupees.

Abhi asked him, 'Do you know its real worth? Must be around three to four hundred rupees. In the name of overheads and brand cost, the price is hiked almost ten times and marked up as three thousand. We are well aware of this and never go for branded stuff. You know, similar things are available at Chandni Chowk also but at much lower prices. After all, what's in a brand?'

They moved on and decided it was time for lunch. Since they ate at the food court in the basement of the mall, they did not hear the rain. The loud music blaring from the speakers also drowned out the sound of the downpour. Finally, when they stepped out, they were in for a shock. They found themselves stranded. The roads were flooded and traffic had come to a standstill. Drenched to the bone, they had to wait for hours to get to the Metro station.

'What happened?' A worried Rekha enquired, looking at the three boys who had just got back home.

Instead of answering her, Ravi asked Shekhar in an agitated tone, 'Mamaji, is this the capital city or a catchment area? One single downpour has inundated every inch of this place. There's so much waterlogging here. It looks as if there are no drains or that they are all clogged. We got caught in massive traffic jams. We even saw some vehicles floating in the water like boats. Trying to reach the Metro station from the Saket malls was a total nightmare. We had a terrible day.'

Shekhar coolly answered his question, 'You've rightly said that Delhi is a catchment area. Well, flooding and water-logging are not alien to us. It's a common feature every year and Delhiites take it as a *chalta hai* matter.'

An irritated Ravi asked, 'Why, Mamaji? Are people not paying taxes? What's the government doing with the money?'

Shekhar explained, 'All this flooding and the resulting traffic jams are man-made. And this goes on even when hundred crore public money is provided in the budget just for de-silting the drains in the city.

'You know, before the onset of every monsoon, the municipality is expected to de-silt all the drains so that the streets are not flooded. The municipal authorities once decided that they would pay a contractor for the quantity of silt that's removed and also for transporting it to the designated dumping place on the outskirts of the city at Ghazipur. At that site, the silt would be weighed on a weigh-bridge and the payment would be made accordingly. A very logical and fair arrangement.

'But what really happens is appalling. We found this out through a confidential informant. He said that the contractor carried the dug-up earth and rubble from a construction site three kilometres away from Ghazipur and claimed it was silt from Rohini. Dishonest engineers endorsed his claim to clear his bills. We trusted our informant and fixed up a sting operation. Since these activities happen only at night, our officers shadowed the contractor and the engineers for three nights.

'One team, equipped with a video camera in their vehicle, stationed themselves close to the construction site. Excavators were digging up the earth and loading the dumpers. These dumpers would leave the site, carrying rubble and mud. Empty dumpers that returned were refilled. Our officers recorded everything and kept a tally of all dumpers. It went on for the whole night. Every time a loaded dumper left the place, our officers passed on the information along with their registration numbers to their colleagues via their mobile phones. Their colleagues followed the dumpers to Ghazipur. The officers made recordings ensuring that the vehicles' registration numbers were clearly visible. The exercise was repeated on the following two nights.

'After the third night, all records at the weigh-bridge were seized. Everything became clear. All the vehicles that had left the construction site loaded with rubble on those three nights were recorded at the dumping place as having brought silt from Rohini.'

'What was done with the evidence collected so painstakingly?' asked Pradeep.

Shekhar replied, 'A case was registered and the engineers and the contractor were taken to the police lock-up and investigations were carried out quickly. It was found that the man had got a contract for de-silting the drains in Rohini. However, no de-silting done was done. Nor was there any transportation of silt from Rohini. So, the drains at Rohini remained unattended and false claims were made using the rubble from the construction site. Public money was being conveniently embezzled by the evil Bakasurs.

'Mind you, the contractor was getting a double benefit—payment for excavating and transporting the rubble as well as a share of the de-silting budget. Look at the audacity of the engineers and the contractors! Surely, they can't be so brazen without the support of their political patrons...Now, do you see why Delhi is flooded when it rains?' Shekhar asked his irate nephew.

By that time, the rain had stopped. The sudden downpour had flooded the city and thrown life into disarray but it had also brought relief from the blistering heat that had been plaguing Delhi for several days. When Abhi pointed this out, Ravi agreed that the rain had its uses as well. But he was not going to forget the flooding and the de-silting fraud that easily. He reasoned, 'Mamaji, could it be because the city is too huge and has so many housing colonies and condominiums as well as slums that it's become impossible to control it?'

Shekhar rubbished this, saying, 'No. The city's size and expansion are not the reasons for the failure. There are even bigger cities in the world that are managed in a far better way. It only requires commitment, which is missing here because of the greed of our Bakasurs. For such people, the city's size works as a boon; it yields more money. Can you imagine the wealth the city generates for those who give permission for construction projects, the engineers who regulate these and their political bosses as well as the police who keep tabs on such activities and inform the municipal authorities?'

Shekhar was interrupted by his orderly, who walked in to inform him that a couple of his officers had arrived to consult him on an urgent matter. A charge-sheet had to be filed on the following day since the sixty days of custody of a Deputy Commissioner and an accused engineer would get over by then. He told the orderly to make the officers comfortable. He would join them in a minute.

Ravi was scowling at his plate and Rekha asked him, 'What's the matter, Ravi? Is something wrong with the food?'

His serious expression morphing into a smile, Ravi said, 'No, Mami. The food is excellent. I'm only trying to guess how much an engineer earns illegally.'

Shekhar laughed along with the others. He said, 'They're stinking rich; every engineer here is a multi-millionaire. For every floor constructed, whether legally or illegally, a price is fixed. Every flat on a floor costs a minimum of one lakh as bribe. Each layout has its own rate. And politicians, who are well-aware of the demands of these engineers, always get their choice officers posted in their areas so that they can get their cut of the bribe without any hassle. And, for this reason, even illegal colonies spring up overnight. And then, in the name of the regularization of such colonies for votes in return, politicians also swindle the funds meant for their development.

'And as for the police, no piece of construction work misses the attention of the local police. The moment it begins, the local police will accuse them of dumping construction materials and causing obstruction to the flow of traffic and the movement of people. In case of illegal construction, the police would intimidate them by threatening to send a report to the municipal authorities. A bargain would be made and they would collect their dues. This is an open secret.

'As far as illegal construction is concerned, we can't say that the people involved are victimized. They collude with the officials anyway. Therefore, they should be taken to task. But when the construction is perfectly legal and without any irregularities, we certainly need to sympathize with them,' Shekhar said.

He quickly finished his dinner and stepped out of the room to meet his officers.

By the time he was done with the discussions with his officers and had given the finishing touches to the charge-sheet, everybody had moved to the lawn. He joined them. Looking at Rekha, who had been meticulously following the case all these days, he heaved a sigh of relief. 'At last, the case against the all-powerful Deputy Commissioner has been completed.'

'Good, you've been racing against time. Now, I'm sure there's no escape for him,' Rekha said with a smile.

'Yes, he will not be able to step out of jail until the trial is over. And the judge is eager to start it soon,' Shekhar assured her.

Pradeep could not stop himself from asking, 'Would you mind telling us the details of the case of the Deputy Commissioner if it is not a secret. What offence has he committed?'

'Now that the case is being sent to the court for trial there is no secret at all. But it's a long story. Since it's already late, why don't we talk about it some other time?' Shekhar asked his curious nephew.

'We'll be leaving the day after tomorrow. Why not tell us right now?' Ravi pleaded.

'Ok, let me have my coffee first,' Shekhar agreed. Sipping it, he began to share the details of the case.

'A while ago, Montek Singh, who owned a farm house, came to me in a totally dejected mood and complained, "Sir, I've been suffering for the past one year. I lost my business since the time they sealed my farm house for want of certain documents though there was no irregularity on my part. Even when I produced them, the Deputy Commissioner was not ready to unseal it. He demanded two crores from me. When I went to the CBI with my complaint, they asked me to bring thirty or forty lakhs so that they could trap him. "I couldn't arrange for the money to trap him. Since my business was sealed, my earnings had dried up. There was no one I could turn to."

Feeling sorry for him, I assured him, "Don't worry. It's possible to catch the Deputy Commissioner without investing any money." Hearing that, the old man was speechless. He was very relieved and his eyes sparkled with hope. He eagerly enquired what he had to do thereafter.

He was given the plan and the script—everything that happened had to be recorded for gathering the evidence needed. Patiently, he tried to take in the instructions. Then, his face glowing with confidence, he ambled out of our office.

Very soon, spy cameras began functioning in his office room. He rehearsed his lines and tested the equipment. He felt sure of himself so he got in touch with the engineer, the assistant of the Deputy Commissioner, and invited him for lunch on a Saturday. He waited for the day to dawn.

Singh was restless from the morning itself, thinking of the lines he had to say, the acting he had to do and the plan he had to stick to. The engineer arrived dot on time for lunch. The drama began. And the recording too started.

Singh welcomed him with a supplicant *namaste*, "Sir, please accept my apology first."

The engineer looked suspicious. "Don't bother. Now, tell why you have called me here."

Singh continued to act apologetic. "Sir, I'm sorry for whatever happened. Realizing I have committed the greatest blunder of my life, I decided to get back to you though belatedly. The loss suffered for the past year can't be made up. But I don't want to suffer any longer. I know very well how large-hearted you and your Deputy Commissioner are. I've learnt the lesson about how vulnerable I'm without your support. I want to run my business. It is for this reason that I have requested you to meet me for lunch. I'm really grateful you responded to my invite."

Delighted at the turn of events, the engineer smiled at him. Looking at Singh who was apologizing again, he relaxed and started a friendly chat. They talked about the good old days of Singh's business as well as his losses. Meanwhile, the table was laid and they settled down to eat.

As they ate, Singh smartly began to insert the script he had rehearsed many a time. He said, "Sir, when your Deputy Commissioner demanded two crores for unsealing, my short-tempered son flew off the handle. It was my mistake that I didn't intervene at that time. For that, I've suffered. I admit that you are the real authorities. Without your support, we have nothing. I've come to terms with it. I'll do whatever you command me to do."

The old man reminded him, "Sir, even when you scaled down the demand to one crore, I didn't realize that it was time to say yes." He nodded his head umpteen times showing his exasperation at his own conduct and said, "Again, let me apologize to you and to the Deputy Commissioner." The engineer looked very pleased, unaware that he had fallen into a trap.

When Singh recalled the dinner they had had at Casino restaurant where delicious prawns were served in huge quantities, the engineer remembered that too. He even recollected the fact that at the time he had proposed that an advance of twenty lakh rupees would serve the purpose of continuing with the dialogue. Singh carried on with his act, "I still regret that I didn't accept that offer. Anyway, forget the past. Please pardon me and my son for our mistakes, engineer *Saheb*. With my head bowed, I'm in front of you, seeking your blessings. Please ensure that the Deputy Commissioner also blesses me."

The engineer told him, "Ok. Let's leave the past behind. I'll try my best to convince the Deputy Commissioner and convey your message to him. Let's be friends again…I'll be in touch with you."

Singh implored the engineer, "Sir, if you can help me, I'll personally touch the feet of the Deputy Commissioner to seek his pardon."

Overwhelmed by the suggestion, the engineer hugged him, saying, "Sure, I'll try my best."

'The man turned out to be a wily old fox. And the engineer fell in the dragnet, right?' Ravi asked.

'He's an intelligent businessman. Moreover, at that time he was desperately waiting for some relief. He had to act. And he did it well,' Shekhar commended Singh.

'Then what happened?' asked Pradeep eagerly.

'The evidence collected so far was very good. And we waited for the recording of the direct conversation between Singh and the Deputy Commissioner to clinch the proof against him also. And it happened soon. On that day, Singh left his office after checking the button camera he had kept concealed behind his tie. He knew that once he switched it on every word would be recorded. For recording faces, he only had to shuffle his tie occasionally. He felt confident that he had adequately rehearsed it.

At the office of the Deputy Commissioner, the engineer received him with a broad smile and a warm embrace and even offered him tea. As they were chatting, the old Sikh requested the engineer, "Sir, I find it difficult to pay twenty lakhs as advance at one go. Can you help me to bring it down to ten lakhs?"

The engineer's pleasant mood instantly changed to exasperation. "Don't renege on your word now. I have already told the Deputy Commissioner about it…Anyway, you may try your luck when you meet him."

The engineer ushered Singh into a large chamber. The Deputy Commissioner stood up with a smile and extended his hand. But, instead, the old man tried to touch his feet, offering his apologies. The smile still intact on his face, the Deputy Commissioner said, "Sardar-*ji*, please don't say sorry. We're like brothers." The old man said, "Thanks for saying that, Commissioner *Saheb.*" He sat down on the seat offered to him. They started to chat.

Again, acting as if he was cringing, Singh said, "Sir,

I'm terribly sorry for whatever has happened. It was a serious mistake on my part. My grumpy son had reacted in an immature way when you had asked for two crore rupees for unsealing our farm house." He checked to see if there was any inkling of suspicion on the officer's face. Finding none, he confidently continued his play acting, "Sir, it was also my mistake not to have made amends for it. But now that your engineer has paved the way for a smooth deal, let's move ahead. He told me that with twenty lakh rupees as advance, we can proceed."

"Yes, yes. There is no point in cribbing about the past. I am a happy-go-lucky, large-hearted man. Forgive and forget is the motto I follow. Let's move on."

After a pause, again speaking in a very submissive tone, Singh said, "Sir, though I'm getting ready for that, I have a special request to make. Now that my business has suffered a lot, have mercy on me."

The Deputy Commissioner was taken aback. Though he spoke in a polite tone, there was a tinge of suspicion when he asked, "Do you think the deal will work out at all?"

Singh feigned sincerity by folding his hands, "Sir, please, I will be devastated if you doubt my sincerity. Our deal will certainly go through. But I'm humbly begging you to take into consideration my present financial position."

Composing himself, the canny officer said, "It's okay. In that case, I suggest that you should meet my engineer and settle the matter."

"Sir, I'll do that. Thanks again for being so generous. We'll meet very soon. May I leave now?"

"Sure," the Deputy Commissioner stood up. Patting Singh on the back and flashing all his teeth, he repeated, "We're like brothers."

Thanking him profusely, the wily old man left the chamber.

When he met the engineer again and repeated his request, he firmly retorted, "No way. Our Deputy Commissioner wouldn't accept anything less than twenty lakhs. Therefore, I cannot help you."

Pretending to be helpless, the old man told him, "Sir, in that case, I'll somehow arrange for the money and meet you soon."

His eyes bright with anticipation, the engineer accompanied Singh to his car to see him off.'

'Good work by the Sardar-*ji*. So, what action was taken then?' Suman was keen to know.

'The evidence collected was more than adequate. That very day, with a case registered against them, the two began cooling their heels in the lock-up. Not only that. Very soon, with his premises unsealed, Singh happily resumed his business activities. The story ended happily for him,' Shekhar said.

'Good!' said a relieved Pradeep. 'How long were the two in custody?'

'For a good amount of time. As long as there are fair judges, there is reason to hope…Court orders are not only binding, but they also stoke the fear of contempt of court. Despite this, there is collusion with criminal elements and widespread corruption as well as apathy on the part of the authorities. Many poor people in Delhi sleep on the streets in the bitterly cold winters but the people in charge of their welfare are not bothered. The officials in charge wake up from their slumber only when the courts slap orders on them. That's when night shelters spring up overnight. Even the killer blue line buses were phased out only because of the courts. Similarly, the police swing into action on pending complaints only when the courts intervene. Corruption blinds the authorities and they never do the right thing unless the courts step in.'

Ravi exclaimed, 'How pathetic all this is!'

Shekhar had to agree. He could not sugarcoat reality for the sake of the youngsters. He wished them goodnight and left the room.

Ravi marvelled at Shekhar's memory after he was gone. 'Mamaji remembers every single case in such minute detail. That's really impressive!'

Abhi said, 'That's true. He doesn't forget a thing. But whosoever handles any matter with full involvement would find it hard to forget the details easily. These things are etched on their mind for life unless they are affected by memory loss.'

He shared an anecdote he had heard from a psychiatrist working at AIIMs. 'Two old couples used to get together regularly to have a meal and a chat. One day, one of them started praising the food at a restaurant he and his wife had visited. "Oh! Really, what's its name?" asked the other man. The first man tried hard to recall the name but it escaped him. He said, "Tell me the name of a flower with a lovely fragrance." The second man said, "Chameli." "Yes. That's it," the first man said. Turning to his wife, he asked, "Chameli, what's the name of the restaurant we went to the other night?"'

They smiled at the vagaries of human memory. It could certainly play a lot of tricks on you if it wanted!

Day Eight

'Look at the sky,' Abhi said, peering out of the window. 'My hunch is that it'll rain soon,' he predicted.

'Should we go for our morning walk or not?' asked Ravi.

'Let's take a chance,' said Pradeep.

They got dressed and stepped out. When they were half-way, thunder clouds began gathering, threatening the city with a downpour. They had to scurry back. Before they could get home, the clouds erupted. It began to pour and all three of them were soaked.

Suman chided them when they got home, 'You shouldn't have gone out when you knew it was sure to rain. Take these towels and dry yourself. Change your clothes quickly or you'll catch a cold.'

Mumbling apologies under their breath, they hurriedly went to their room to change.

It rained continuously for two hours and the

roads were flooded. Perhaps it would go on raining forever...Shekhar informed them that the forecast said it would rain till evening. Disappointed, the boys dropped their plans to go out that day. At their request, Shekhar stayed back at home and watched television with them. Their pets stayed put under the bed, scared of the thunder and the rain.

The Kedarnath disaster had hit the headlines of all the national dailies that day. TV channels broadcast reports about it non-stop, competing to stay ahead of each other by sharing sensational details. A cloudburst centered on the State of Uttarakhand had caused massive floods and landslides resulting in the loss of several lives and extensive damage to the landscape. This was one of the worst natural disasters India had faced in recent history. News reports stressed on the fact that experts had been apprehensive about this disaster for quite some time. The Central government and State officials were flayed for not paying heed to their repeated warnings. It was reported that the District Magistrate had suffered a heart attack after the disaster wrecked the State.

Engrossed in watching the macabre dance of death in Uttarakhand, Ravi asked, 'Mamaji, it looks like this disaster is manmade. It could've been avoided had the proper precautions been taken?'

'It may not be deliberate, Ravi,' Shekhar said. 'But in their selfishness to promote their own interests, if anyone condoned deforestation and approved unviable projects even after the experts objected to them, they certainly have a hand in it. Perhaps due to complacence or ignorance, they may have thought it was fine to ignore the experts. Anyway, it's for the CBI to establish the facts of the matter now.'

'Are you sure that the CBI would do a decent job?' Ravi asked. 'It's doubtful, isn't it? People keep saying that the CBI is not all that keen to deal with corruption in high places.'

The rain battered the windows and the wind went on howling like a wild thing. Shekhar said, 'You have a point. There have been many flip-flops on the part of the CBI during investigations.'

Citing the instance of the Taj corridor case levelled against former Uttar Pradesh chief minister Mayawati, he explained:

'It was a project of Rs 175 crore to upgrade tourist facilities near the Taj Mahal during her tenure as chief minister of UP. An FIR was registered with the allegation of embezzlement. But the pace of the CBI probe changed from time to time depending on her allegiance with the ruling party at the Centre. The probe was slow at times, very fast at other times and often accompanied by flip-flops.'

Ravi remarked, 'Perhaps this why the Supreme Court commented that the CBI is a caged parrot of the government. It seems to be deferential to corrupt politicians and is afraid to be unbiased.'

'Yes, the Supreme Court was right to pass that scathing remark. Why shy away from speaking the truth?' commented Shekhar.

He paused for a moment and then cited instances of when the CBI had succumbed to political pressure. 'I'm aware of how one CBI officer whitewashed a complaint in the matter of sewerage management in the city by the Delhi Jal Board. I'd prepared the report after a long study. Hundreds of crores of rupees were swindled by some officials of the Board by astronomically inflating the budget and by committing several irregularities. Though there was a very clear case for prosecuting the officials, the matter was closed. In spite of the fact that the Delhi Jal Board is a cesspool of corruption, it's so powerful and influential that no case is ever taken up against those officials.

'Here's another glaring example. Take the case of Rajashekhar Reddy, the former CM of Andhra Pradesh. As long as he and his son were in the good books of the Congress Party's High Command, whatever they did was acceptable. Once Reddy died and his son demanded the post of CM, everything changed. The same Congress Party that had protected the father and son began to accuse the Reddy family of corruption. The CBI toed the line of the ruling party in this case. If the Reddys were corrupt, they were always corrupt. It was the job of the CBI to have taken action against them long back while CM Reddy was allegedly swindling the State of thousands and thousands of crores. The irony is that when belated action is taken against the Bakasurs, people side with them. Many voters behave as if they are the only great leaders around capable of being in power. It looks like criminality and corruption have become added qualifications for leaders.'

Television channels cut back and forth from the Kedarnath disaster to the incessant rain and resulting chaos on Delhi streets. The downpour had brought life to a screeching halt in the capital. Reports showed the slum-dwellers on the banks of the Yamuna being hurriedly shifted to safer places fearing that the river would rise above the danger mark.

Shekhar lamented, 'People still hanker for corrupt dynasties as if the country is bankrupt of good leadership. There are too many high-profile cases in which the powerful and the well-connected try to influence the course of the CBI's investigations through the government. Fortunately, at times, the CBI bosses have made amends after taking incorrect decisions. Let me tell you about one such case.'

He gave a brief account of it to the boys. This was an instance of fraud committed by Mohammad Ali, a well-connected Chief Commissioner of Central Exercise.

'In two matters involving tax violations by

entrepreneurs, the upright Central Exercise officers showed no mercy and slapped huge fines on them. The entrepreneurs came in to appeal before Ali who was the appellate authority of the department. There was a set procedure—the appeal should be taken on record first, then be heard; and at the time of hearing, it was necessary that the lower authority was also properly represented in the matter on behalf of the department. In course of time, Ali heard the appeals and issued orders in favour of the entrepreneurs.

'Later, a very specific and confidential piece of information was received by the CBI that Ali had colluded with those entrepreneurs and issued the orders from his house after he had been transferred. Therefore, criminal cases were registered and investigations were carried out. This led to several revelations.

'First, even if the plan was to take the appeal on record in October, Ali recorded the month as March in the register crammed with daily entries. He adjusted the entry as (b) of serial number 28 in one case and as (c) of serial number 28 in the other.

'Then he planned the date of hearing. Initially, he showed 13 October as the date of hearing. But he received the transfer order dated 12 October. Obviously, he could not hear the appeal and so he changed it to 10 October. This date also did not suit him because of the nuances involved. Then he altered it to 3 October. Let me tell you that all these alterations by the shameless man were made by erasing existing entries with a whitener and rewriting them. He went ahead and issued orders favouring the defaulters in both cases. This happened after he was relieved from his post.

'Now, look at the evidence. The entries in the register that featured the appeals with serial numbers 28(b) and 28(c) were clearly suspicious. Then, the alteration of the dates was confirmed via infra-red examination by experts. More importantly, it was found that the depositions of the two officers who were supposed to have represented the department were fabricated since both of them were undergoing a training course at the time of hearing. After the findings came to light, all the investigating officers and their superiors recommended that Ali should be prosecuted.

'But, in course of time, the CBI Headquarters opined that the material on record was not adequate enough to prosecute him and issued orders to close both the cases. Everyone was shocked. There was a wave of protests demanding that the evidence collected with a great deal of effort and expense was not wasted and a thoroughly dishonest officer was not given the benefit of the doubt. The CBI finally conceded.'

Ravi asked, 'Mamaji, the officers at the CBI

Headquarters must be senior people and more experienced than most others, right? They also have expert senior legal advisors there to guide them?'

'That's right.'

'Then, why did they reject the evidence and issue orders to close those cases in the first place? If there were no strong protests, Ali would have got off scot-free.'

'True. The answer is simple—pressure exerted by the powerful,' said Shekhar.

The boys looked disappointed.

Shekhar added, 'There are some brilliant officers at the CBI who conduct thorough investigations. The CBI gets its reputation thanks to these remarkable officers. Unfortunately, people forget the good work they do when new scams surface and the Bakasurs among them take charge of investigations.'

'The Bakasurs who are looting the country at will are the stumbling blocks on the path to development,' Ravi said. 'The real enemies of the nation.'

Shekhar smiled at his nephew warmly. 'Well put, Ravi,' he said. 'You know that spiritually exalted people try to realize their *atma* (self) so as to become good human beings and come closer to the *Paramatma* (God). Unlike them, these Bakasurs interpret "self" as pure selfishness and grab every opportunity to help no one but themselves.'

'True, Mamaji. They have no real concern for

the poor,' Pradeep said. 'They collude with mining lobbies to rob tribals of their land and resources. Furious and desperate, many of these people become Naxals and take up arms.'

Shekhar said, 'As I've told you, the only solution to all our problems is letting independent entities like Lokpal and Lokayuktas promptly and effectively deal with corruption at the top. As a consequence, there'll be checks on the brazen corruption infecting the lower ranks as well.'

Pradeep asked, 'Do you think the media is doing a good job of exposing corruption? Freedom of the press is a right guaranteed by the Constitution. Is this right under threat, Mamaji?'

Shekhar replied, 'The media may be doing a good job in some cases but certainly not in all of them. It is said that the freedom of the press is restricted to the pleasure of the publishers. Do you know who the publishers are? Most of them are business people and industrialists. Do you think their equations with the government are absolutely above board? No. The government can issue orders to them and journalists will be made to toe the line when reporting about the powerful and their scams. It's just like an honest government servant, whose freedom to work impartially is restricted by the corrupt seniors in their departments. And of course, there are black sheep among journalists as well. They collude with the corrupt or use the evidence they have gathered to intimidate them and make a fast buck. We should therefore not place too much hope on a free press.'

Pradeep said, 'Even when it comes to politicians, I think there is a small percentage of honest people in their ranks. It's the corrupt ninety-nine percent that make the rest seem bad. Perhaps the percentage is a bit different for bureaucrats.'

Shekhar smiled. 'My hope is that youngsters like you have the power to bring about change. You're unique. You can turn things around.'

Day Nine

Ravi glanced at his watch. Their bags were packed. They were just a couple of hours away from boarding the train to Bhopal. He would miss his uncle, his cousin and his aunt. The last few days had been truly memorable. He wished he could stay on for longer and have more conversations with his uncle.

Looking at Shekhar, he said, 'Mamaji, thanks to all of you, we've had an excellent stay. We've seen so many great sights and learned so much. You've taught us many important facts about the lives of the rich and the poor, the corrupt and the upright; the cracks in the system; corruption and pigs and illegal wealth…More importantly, we know all about the Bakasurs destroying the nation now.'

Shekhar was very moved. 'I'm glad you came to stay with us,' he said. 'If my words influence you and inspire you to work for change, I'll be the happiest man on earth.'

'Absolutely, Mamaji,' Ravi said. 'In fact, I'm planning to share our experiences and your stories with our friends via social media. Pradeep may also do the same.'

'That's wonderful!' Shekhar exclaimed. 'Do me a favour if you can. Let people know about Bakasurs and the pigs who wallow in dirty money. That's the first step to change. Information is power. Only an informed public can bring about change in our country.'

'Our mission is to make "Bakasur" the brand name for every single corrupt man,' Pradeep announced.

'Absolutely,' Shekhar nodded his head vigorously.

'Then, we will kickstart a campaign,' the boys said in unison.

'We dream of the day when Bakasurs will vanish from the face of the earth for good,' Ravi said.

Pradeep added, 'Ravi, you know, a dream is not what you see in your sleep. It's the thing that doesn't let you sleep.'

Shekhar approved of his jovial nephew's poetic definition. Suman looked on as the boys and Abhi and began to cart their bags to the waiting car. When everyone got in, Pradeep suddenly rushed back indoors as if he had forgotten something. He ran straight to the pets, patted them and bid goodbye to them. 'My sweet friends, we had a nice time with you. Take care.'

They wagged their tails and licked his hand. They were going to miss him.

Shekhar, Rekha and Abhi accompanied them to the station. They parted with warm hugs and fond goodbyes on the platform.

'I'll be waiting to hear from you. Stay in touch,' Shekhar told the boys as they boarded the train.

'Sure, Mamaji,' they chorused.

Standing at the door of their compartment, the boys showed him the thumbs-up sign and shouted, 'Bakasurs *murdabad* (down with Bakasurs). Bharat *zindabad* (long live India).' Many people looked at them, surprise writ large on their faces. The boys were all charged up and they did not care about the looks they were getting. They waved at Shekhar, Abhi and Rekha one last time as the train gained speed and pulled out of the station.

Epilogue

I

A few days later, Shekhar sent an e-mail to his nephews. After reading it, Ravi and Pradeep would share it with their friends and classmates and make sure it circulated widely. The two of them had formed a progressive organization called Young Men's Brigade that had already garnered a thousand members and was gaining strength day by day. The group had uploaded the names of 5,000 Bakasurs from among their relatives and friends online.

Subject: Bharat *zindabad*. Bakasurs *murdabad*.

I hope your campaign against the Bakasurs of our time is growing. In the meanwhile, I want to tell you that we have something to celebrate.

Maybe you've already read about it in the papers. Recently, the Supreme Court gave a twin blow to the political class through two landmark verdicts. These orders should bring great relief to the country and rid politics of criminals. Hats off to the exemplary Lily Thomas and the Jan Chaukidar activist Basant Kumar Choudhary!

First, the judgement in the Lily Thomas petition has ended the dream-run of convicted legislators. All these years, they conveniently took advantage of the provision in section 8(4) of the Representation of the People Act that such people could retain their seats for three months or till the final disposal of their appeals. Now, the court has not only struck down such relief but also debarred them from contesting the next election even if their appeals are pending in higher court. Isn't that great?

Also, giving a deadlier punch to the political class, the Supreme Court has upheld the Patna High Court in the Jan Chaukidar petition. In their verdict, they extended the ambit of Section 62(5) of the Representation of People Act that no person shall vote in any election if he/she is confined in a prison, whether under a sentence of imprisonment or transportation or otherwise, or is in the lawful custody of the police. They ruled that when a person is disqualified from being a voter, he/she is not qualified to contest the election to the House of the people or the Legislative Assembly of a State. The Court rightly asked, 'If a person under detention is not allowed to vote, how can he be allowed to contest?' Absolutely logical, isn't it?

Kudos to them! The judges have done a great service to the nation.

These are certainly the first steps to cleanse our electoral system. Perhaps good days are certainly ahead for our country and our democracy. Sorry for my slip! We're still not a real democracy. We should probably call it an oligarchy since the legacy of the Bakasurs is sure to be passed on to their equally corrupt children. These neo-dynasties are power hungry monsters. Obviously, being used to witnessing the unscrupulous activities of their fathers, they would have no hesitation in filling their shoes and perpetuating their misrule and misdeeds. Otherwise, how can one explain the suspension of Durga, an honest and pro-active young IAS officer, for taking on the Noida sand mafias for their illegal operations when their collusion with the Bakasurs in the government is obvious?

Like many others, I'm tired of political vendetta and misuse of power. With almost every party pampering and patronizing criminal and corrupt elements, we've had enough. Surely, the two judgements I mentioned will bring about a change.

Politicians have been trying to come up with

ways to counter the laudable order of the Central Information Commission that requires them to declare all donations that their parties receive. Plans are on to amend the law regarding donations as well. The fact that many politicians oppose this move shows how murky their deals are. They resist any reform that demands transparency. Now, with these judgments in affect, they are scared and are contemplating going in for an appeal or initiating remedial legislative action to establish the supremacy of the Parliament. They only want to perpetuate their misrule. We live in the hope that the judiciary will find a way to thwart their attempts.

We shouldn't despair. The two Supreme Court judgements I mentioned have brought a smile to the faces of millions of people in our corruption-ridden, fraud-filled and criminalized polity. When there are such judges with a conscience gracing the court, there is indeed reason to smile.

We should celebrate now because the judgements will make sure that criminals will no longer be able to wield power. They won't be able to whitewash their lies and claim to be leaders of the people. Hopefully, the governments of dynasties and of the oligarchy will also be a thing of the past sooner or later when the country is in the safe hands of dedicated and honest leaders. A strong Lokpal would then come into existence and drive the greedy Bakasurs out of governance. And our country will be able to cherish true democracy then.

With hopes for a better and brighter future.

Love,

Mamaji

II

Years had flown by. Pradeep and Ravi were shaping up as young professionals and their Anti-Bakasur Brigade (ABB), which was free of political affiliations, was going from strength to strength. The organization had a strong presence in every district in their home state.

AAB was planning to hold a protest march on Sunday. They wanted to ensure a large turnout for the protest since a week ago, a few ABB activists had been arrested during a peaceful protest. ABB was demanding the immediate arrest of all those involved in a multi-crore nutrition scam. The CAG had found out that fake figures had been submitted regarding the women and children who were the intended beneficiaries of the scheme. Fake numbers of scooters, tankers, etc., in place of the actual tally of transport vehicles were also used. The scamsters had siphoned off thousands of crores of public funds. The CM's name figured at the top of the list of suspects and the State government was trying to pin the blame on a clerical error.

On Friday, a meeting was held at the ABB office to discuss the arrangements for the protest march. Office bearers and volunteers expressed their thoughts freely. Ravi and Pradeep were active participants in the meeting. Their uncle and mentor, Shekhar, was on his way to Bhopal to visit them. Soon after the meeting, the two of them planned to rush to the station to welcome their Mamaji.

The President of the State Unit of ABB, senior advocate Sanjay Arora, was the first to speak at the meeting. 'Fighting corruption is a hackneyed phrase that the ruling party parrots,' he said. 'But what is actually being done to bring about change? The Rafael deal is being treated as a clear case of corruption and cronyism by French investigators but the government has stalled even the preliminary enquiry by the CBI in India by amending the anti-corruption law itself. An impartial enquiry would have exposed all those involved. The Rs 50,000 crore Krishna-Godavari gas basin fraud allegation against Mukesh Ambani was hushed up by snatching away the Anti-Corruption Bureau from the Delhi government. It is common knowledge that the electoral bonds scheme was designed to facilitate anonymous corporate funding to political parties. Under political pressure, the Supreme Court, the highest court in the land, delays dealing with critical matters like the Pegasus software case that violated the privacy of several Indian citizens.

Institutions like the Directorate of Enforcement and the CBI are at the beck and call of the government. This is a very safe environment for people indulging in crime and corruption to jump on the bandwagon of the ruling party.'

Prakash, a journalist who was an active member of ABB, commented, 'Forget about taking action against the Bakasurs supporting the ruling party. Neither the media nor leaders speak about the rampant corruption in the country. When drugs worth thousands of crores are caught at Adani's Mudra port, no one's penalized. Sainthood is conferred on the corrupt who are close to those in power. And the media meekly toes the line.'

'You're right,' said Sharmila, a senior lecturer in physics. 'There is also an alarming tendency to disregard scientific principles. Remember how scientists were puzzled when the PM said that clouds would prevent radars from detecting passing aircraft and gas from gutters can be used for cooking. Such unscientific remarks are reported verbatim. Economists are confused to hear our finance minister say that the record fall of the rupee against the dollar should be read as the dollar going strong and not as the rupee weakening. Foreign investors are reluctant to invest in India due to the lack of confidence in our political leadership. Thus, our economy is adversely affected.'

'And that is such a shame,' said Abdul Karim,

a professor of economics. 'Dubious policy decisions are being forcefully implemented almost daily. For example, demonetization, which was thrust upon the country has proved to be a disaster since all the black money of the rich found its way back into the banks. This measure, coupled with the hurriedly implemented GST has only helped crony capitalists, while the backbone of our economy, the MSMEs were decimated, resulting in unprecedented unemployment figures. The farm laws and the non-implemented minimum procurement prices were designed to favour the corporate sector. More and more privatization has led to the rich becoming richer. Crores of public money lent by banks to crony capitalists is being waived.'

'The issue is the leadership's will to fight corruption,' stressed Soha, a final year engineering student. 'What message does it send out when the party in power purchases MLAs with crores? Who is prosecuting the businessmen who defrauded the nation and fled to foreign countries with thousands of crores? Over eighty crore Indians are surviving on free rations while defaulters and scamsters flourish.'

Ravi said, 'We must take up all these issues at our march. Corruption is on our agenda. And so is blatant discrimination based on religious grounds. When a girl was recently killed by accident by the Chinese *manja* (kite-flying thread) of a boy, the houses of the poor retail sellers in the area were bulldozed since they were Muslims, but the wholesale seller, who was a Hindu right-wing activist was left untouched. Hindu beef exporters are never questioned but many poor Muslim beef traders are inhumanly lynched. Fanatics and extremists who spread hatred among different communities are being protected by those in power.'

Pradeep was furious. 'These lumpen elements have become so bold that they even deify Godse, who killed Mahatma Gandhi. They must be reined in before they destroy the whole country.'

Adv. Arora agreed with him. 'They are bent on tearing us apart. For such people, Savarkar and Shyama Prasad Mukherjee, who enjoyed the largesse of the British for feeding them information against our freedom fighters, are icons. It's an irony that they are giving us lessons on patriotism and nationalism these days. At our march we need to send out a message, loud and clear, about the dangers they pose.'

When the meeting ended and the plans for the march were firmly in place, Ravi and Pradeep headed to the railway station. Staring at the display screen on the platform, Ravi lamented, 'With every passing day, Bakasurs of various shapes and hues are proliferating in our country.'

Pradeep, who was also scanning the screen for the Delhi train, said, 'It's as if we're under the evil spell of Rahu's curse.' Then, he spotted the train's arrival time on the screen and excitedly announced, 'Mamaji will be here in fifteen minutes.'

They sat down on a bench and waited for Shekhar. How things had changed for the worse in a decade since the time they had been initiated into the fight against corruption by him...

Both of them vividly remembered the day when their Mamaji had sent them an e-mail about two landmark Supreme Court judgements that were meant to curb criminality among the political class. They also recollected the Anna Movement that had demanded an autonomous Lokpal, a body that was independent of the government, which was meant to ensure transparent election funding and fair elections. Hope was not in short supply then. The Anna Movement had also shaped Arvind Kejriwal's ideology and motivated him to form the Aam Admi Party (AAP), a political party that promised corruption-free governance.

But promises had fizzled out. Only a lame-duck Lokpal had been created and the BJP, which had come to power at the Center in 2014 riding a wave of popular sentiment has started to capture power in various States by hook or by crook. AAP, the party that won the election in Delhi with the support of the common man had bagged a landslide victory in Punjab in 2022. The party was aiming for more and showcasing their people-friendly measures all over the country. In the meanwhile, dwarfed by both these parties, and deserted by some of its own power-hungry leaders, the Congress had been steadily shrinking. With the hope of rejuvenating the grand old party, Rahul Gandhi had set out on a 150-day-long Bharat Jodo Yatra, walking from southern India all the way to Kashmir.

The Yatra aimed to unite people against divisive communal politics and to raise questions about people's issues ignored by the ruling party. It had succeeded in galvanizing lakhs of Indians. This was the only silver lining to be found in a gloomy political scenario.

As the train from Delhi came to a screeching halt, the brothers rushed to greet their hero with broad smiles. They touched Shekhar's feet and he hugged both of them. They picked up his bags and walked him to their car. Pradeep offered to drive them home. Shekhar was happy to say yes.

Soon after they got home and Shekhar drank a cup of tea, he settled down to have a chat with his nephews.

'Tell me what you've been up to,' he said. 'What do you see happening around us?'

Pradeep burst out, 'Recent happenings remind me

of the *Panchatantra* story of a jackal who fell into a pit of slush. In awe of his looks, and trusting his claim that he was a mysterious creature with superpowers, the innocent animals of the jungle made him king. They suffered a great deal during his reign of terror. One day, a heavy shower exposed the charlatan and he was chased away. Mark my words. This will happen in our country too. Very soon.'

Ravi was quick to support him. 'There are welcome signs that voters have realized the mistake they committed. False claims and propaganda are being exposed daily. Now, the regime is desperately holding rallies and roadshows to attract the public's attention.'

Sekhar asked, 'Why blame conniving politicians alone? People who vote them to power have to sufferer the consequences, right?'

Ravi said, 'Mamaji, people only wanted a better life when they voted for the BJP. They trusted the party's promise of an idyllic future. Little did they realize that a dark shadow would taint everything—the economy, secularism and social harmony. Many voters were swayed by propaganda. They were not aware that they would face the deadly combination of Meghanaths, Kumbhakarnas and Ravans along with Bakasurs of different varieties when the party came to power. Truthfulness is anathema now and those who stand by the truth is persecuted. No honest person is spared be it officials, judges, civil rights activists or academics.'

Pradeep said, 'Justice Khureshi...

Suman walked in and interrupted him at that moment. 'What are your nephews saying?' she asked Shekhar. 'To me, they sound like angry young men—always thinking and talking about ABB.'

'Suman, I'm really proud of them. Apart from being skilled engineers they're also concerned citizens. In fact, at this juncture, the country needs thousands of such youngsters who can set the right course for society. They have to protect it from criminals and deviants, who are being encouraged by some political forces.'

Suman was glad to hear her brother praising her sons so highly.

Pradeep resumed, 'Justice Khureshi wasn't elevated to the Supreme Court because he was bold enough to be tough with Amit Shah in a murder case. Justice Muralidharan was transferred overnight for ordering an FIR against Anurag Thakur and others within twenty-four hours in the matter of the Delhi riots. Muralidharan is still being persecuted by some Bakasurs who are in power. The mystery of Judge Loya's death remains unresolved or rather the issue is buried in the Supreme Court like many other crucial matters, including electoral bonds, Rafael, Birla-Sahara diary corruption case, etc.'

Shekhar said, 'These are dark times for our country.

Autonomous institutions, including universities, the media and the judiciary are being subjugated. Authoritarianism is masquerading as democracy. When an incident of purchase of legislators comes to light, there is total silence from the leadership. We mutely watch the transmigration of criminal souls to the ruling party. They are granted immunity from legal action for their crimes. Crime and corruption seem to have become the hallmark of politics.'

Pradeep pointed out, 'Many politicians who are facing trial in serious economic offences continue to occupy the post of CM. Corrupt legislators, including those whose who have charges of rape and murder pending against them, refuse to quit.'

'Mamaji, do you see any hope of change?' A desperate Ravi asked.

'We must focus on electoral reforms,' Shekhar replied. 'Unless there is a level playing field, India will end up with one-party rule, which is nothing but fascist authoritarianism by another name.'

Pradeep said, 'I think we've drifted away from the ideals of our Constitution. Instead of focusing on the last man in the queue as Gandhi desired, attention is given only to the rich. Due to our skewed policies, we've almost hit rock bottom in the Hunger Index and have record rates of unemployment. And inflation is out of control.'

'When dictatorship masquerades as democracy

and Bakasurs are running the country, democracy is on its last legs,' Shekhar warned his nephews. 'But there are glimmers of hope. The charges against the UPA government in the 2G scam were subsequently proved to be concocted. And the CAG who submitted the report was shown to be involved in a conspiracy against the UPA government, which had been in power at that time. Rahul Gandhi's Bharat Jodo Yatra has touched a chord with voters. A united opposition could be the solution to our woes. I think sustaining democracy is the first priority for the country now. Through ABB, I urge you to keep up the demand for an autonomous Lokpal that functions independently of the government. Fight for it until it becomes a reality. Equally important is the matter of making election funding totally transparent.'

'What about Arvind Kejriwal's AAP and its promises to fight corruption?'

'Unfortunately, Kejriwal wound up AAP's internal Lokpal after its first fanfare-filled initiation. Furthermore, he hasn't set up an independent Lokpal in Punjab after AAP formed the government there although he has the authority to do so. We'll have to wait and watch to see which direction his party takes...Youngsters like you have to ensure that things change for the better. Only eternal vigilance on your part can save our nation from the Bakasurs who are on the rampage.'

Acknowledgements

Credit goes to:

Rajiv Nishaana for prodding me to write on anti-corruption.

Padmaja, my life partner, for inspiring me.

Mihir Srivastava, my journalist friend for instilling a new life for this publication and for promotion of the concept.

Ravi Singh, Publisher, Speaking Tiger Books, for his perspective and to Vineetha Mokkil, Senior Editor, Speaking Tiger Books, for her painstaking work.

Mohit Suneja for his thoughtful sketches that are bound to leave a lasting impression on readers.